A BROKEN BOND

LECTOR HOUSE PUBLIC DOMAIN WORKS

A BROKEN BOND

NICHOLAS CARTER

ISBN: 978-93-5420-774-7

Published: -

© 2021
LECTOR HOUSE LLP

LECTOR HOUSE LLP
E-MAIL: lectorpublishing@gmail.com

A BROKEN BOND

OR,
THE MAN WITHOUT MORALS

BY

NICHOLAS CARTER

Author of the celebrated stories of Nick Carter's adventures,
which are published exclusively in the New Magnet Library, conceded
to be among the best detective tales ever written.

CONTENTS

A BROKEN BOND

CHAPTER I.

A SHOT FROM AMBUSH.

Behind a big rock which looked down over the wide, straggling road that ran upward through the mountains crouched a long, lean figure. Snuggled against his right shoulder was a rifle, and the bearded face beneath the broad-brimmed panama was turned toward the roadway below. The hot sun beat down remorselessly, and its blinding rays were reflected from the rocks. Perspiration poured down the man's face, and now and then he moved impatiently to brush away some buzzing insect. His head was raised slightly above the level of the rock, and from his point of vantage a splendid panorama spread out beneath him.

To his left lay the mountains, blue, remote, and full of rugged dignity all their own. To his right, a fertile South American valley revealed itself in the shimmering distance. Occasionally, as a light puff of wind came up from the lowlands, it brought with it the dull, heavy noise of an engine at work.

Half an hour passed, and then the first sign of life was revealed in the roadway below. There appeared round a bend a long line of mules, each of them burdened with two big packs. In front of the train of mules walked a white man clad in dingy overalls.

The figure crouching behind the rock moved slightly and seemed to grow tense and expectant, while the eyes in the bearded face glinted as they peered down at the road.

Nothing happened, however. The mules plodded on, with their leader striding away ahead of them, and the lonely sentinel watched them until they had passed down the road and had vanished below the level of the rise which led them on to the plains.

"He ought to be coming soon now."

The man spoke aloud, and there was a curious, metallic sound in his rasping voice.

Ten minutes passed, and then the clear, drumming sound of a horse's hoofs came to him, and presently around the same jagged spur there appeared the figure of a man on horseback. He was riding along at a good pace, but the reins were lying loosely across the horse's neck, and the animal was picking its way unguided down the rough surface of the road. Evidently it was on a familiar trail.

At the sight, the lurking figure grew tenser still, and the sound of a low growl, almost animal-like in character, might have been heard. Slowly the rifle was nestled closer to the shoulder. The panama hat, being too conspicuous, was pulled off and dropped behind him, after which the bare, rather bald head was lowered until the right cheek touched the stock of the gun. The left eye was closed, and the right sighted along the barrel, which at the same time was shifted, following the man on horseback.

A few moments passed, during which the down-pointed muzzle shifted like a spy-glass, following the moving object. Then——

Crack! Into the still air a blue puff of smoke rose and hung for a moment above the rock. The drone of the bullet sounded clearly down the edge of the slope as the deadly missile hurled itself toward its mark. A quick cry came up from the roadway, and the weapon was stealthily withdrawn.

Quickly, however, the man behind the rock peered down, but when he did so he saw that blind chance had stepped in and thwarted him. The horse had apparently stumbled on a loose rock just as the shot was fired, and had reared back slightly to recover its footing; therefore, it was into the animal's soft, rounded neck that the heavy bullet had bored its way, and not into the more precious target at which it had been aimed.

The creature was now lying in the roadway, and the convulsive movements of its limbs could be seen dimly through the little cloud of dust which had been raised by its fall.

The man on the horse's back had been hurled in a heap by the side of the road, but as his would-be murderer watched, he saw him rise to his feet and stare up in the general direction of the rock from which the shot had been fired. Warned by that movement, the skulker swiftly jerked his head back and crouched still lower in his place.

"Curse him!" the hard voice grated. "He always has the fiend's own luck!"

Grasping his rifle and hat, but still keeping on hands and knees, he began instinctively to crawl away under cover of the rock. He had gone no more than a yard, though, before he paused irresolutely and his fingers sought his belt.

There were other bullets in that belt, but the man's failure had unnerved him, and a certain fatalistic instinct told him that he was not likely to succeed in a second attempt, now that the first had come to naught. The figure in the road would be on its guard now, and if another shot missed its mark, the point from which it had been fired would almost certainly be located. From that would only be a step to the discovery of the shooter's identity, and the latter did not care to contemplate such a possibility. Consequently, with a snakelike movement, the lean figure resumed its progress away from the rocks, and presently, having reached the protection of large bowlders, straightened up a little more and increased its pace.

The fugitive knew that the man he had tried to kill was more than usually fond of the dying horse, and would probably delay at its side for a precious minute or two before attempting to solve the mystery of the shot. That delay promised to enable him to make good his escape, and he was resolved to take every possible advantage of it. For perhaps fifteen minutes he doubled and twisted, now ascending and now descending the foothills. At the end of that time he had reached the road again, and, watching his chance, dodged across it. This latest move brought him into thick woods, through which he hurriedly threaded his way in the direction of the valley.

He hid his rifle in a hollow tree, and when he reached the little mining camp he had cunningly concealed all evidence of agitation or guilt.

The knowledge of the act was not destined to remain locked in his own breast, however, as he was soon to learn. At his destination, the Condor Mine, he found Charlie Floyd, the mine's physician, waiting for him, and wearing a very stern expression.

"I have something important to say to you, Mr. Stone," the young doctor said grimly, and led the way to a spot where they were out of earshot.

"What's up?" demanded Stone, who was one of the two original owners of the mine. He and his partner, Winthrop Crawford, had only recently sold out for a cool million.

"Much," was the grave answer. "I happened to be roaming about in the foothills back there a little while ago, and I saw you take that pot shot at Mr. Crawford."

"What are you raving about?" growled Stone, with the greatest apparent surprise.

"I'm not raving at all, Mr. Stone. I always carry field glasses on my walks, as you know, and, being startled by the shot, I looked in that direction, saw the puff of smoke from behind the rock, and leveled my glasses on the spot. I saw you when you looked down to see if the bullet had done its work; saw you as plainly as if you had been not more than ten feet away. There's no possibility of a mistake. I was in a position to watch your movements afterward, and saw you sneaking away. I recognized your hat, too."

Stone had wilted at first when the field glasses were mentioned, but now he seemed to have plucked up fresh courage, and even assumed a defiant attitude.

"Well, what are you going to do about it?" he demanded. "One or the other of us will have to kick the bucket sooner or later. Crawford has it in for me, and I only acted in self-defense. If I don't get him first, he'll get me as sure as fate."

The young physician looked at him searchingly, but there was much more of pity than condemnation in his glance.

"You needn't be afraid that I'm going to give you up to justice, Mr. Stone," he said, after a pause. "You'll resent it, of course, but I'm pretty sure that you're not responsible for your actions. I hold your liberty, if not your life, in my hands, though, and I'm going to name a condition in return for my silence."

CHAPTER II.

THE WITNESS MAKES CONDITIONS.

James Stone assumed a belligerent attitude.

"What do you mean by saying I'm not accountable?" he blustered. "You think I'm crazy?"

"I wouldn't use quite such a harsh word," was the reply. "But I've been watching you for some time, and I'm certain that your mind is slightly affected. This grouch of yours against Mr. Crawford is entirely uncalled-for, and everybody knows it but you. He's the best friend you have in the world, and would do anything and everything for you. Until lately you've been the same toward him, and there's nothing that could have caused such a breach. Mr. Crawford wouldn't harm a hair of your head, and you wouldn't think of harming him if you were yourself."

"Rot!" exclaimed Stone. "You don't know anything about it, Floyd, and it's none of your business; it's nobody's business but ours. Something has come between us, and you'll have to take my word for it that Crawford has got it in for me. He's a deep one. You'd think butter wouldn't melt in his mouth, but all the time he's scheming to finish his old partner. I know, and I'm not going to have any young whipper-snapper tell me to my face that I'm crazy."

Charlie Floyd's lips tightened.

"Would you prefer to be branded as a would-be assassin, Mr. Stone?" he asked cuttingly. "I'm putting the most innocent interpretation I can to your act, and if you know what's good for yourself you'll accept it as the lesser of two evils. You have a great deal more influence here than I have in most ways, but you know that Mr. Crawford is more popular than you. You've lost your popularity in these last few months by your dogged, brooding manner and your harsh words. If I should reveal this attempt of yours on your partner's life, you know perfectly well that it would go hard with you. No one would have any sympathy for you, and you'd get the limit. Just think of that before you call me names, and remember that I have it in my power to break you. Now will you listen to what I have to say?"

The miner moistened his lips and glanced about with shifty eyes.

"I'll listen, Charlie," he said, with a suggestion of a whine in his tone. "It ain't pleasant to be called crazy, you know, but if you'll stand by me I'll make it worth your while."

The young physician knew at once what he meant.

"None of that, Mr. Stone!" he said quickly. "I don't want a cent of your money. I would not keep silent for the whole five hundred thousand they say you received for your half interest in the Condor. I'm making this offer simply for your own good. I really believe you're not responsible for your recent actions, but I feel sure there isn't much the matter with you. For that reason I want to shield you from the consequences if I can, and try to set you on the road to recovery. You and Crawford are going to New York soon, aren't you?"

"That's the plan—by the next boat," was the sullen reply. "We figured it out before this came up, and of course I was anxious to get back home when I'd made my pile. I haven't been back in twenty-five years. When this break came, though, I wasn't keen on going back with Win. But he wouldn't hear of anything else. I reckon he thinks the trip will give him a good chance to polish me off."

"The plan still holds good, then?"

"Yes. I ain't a coward, and if one of us doesn't get the other before, then you won't find me backing out."

Young Floyd's brows were knit, and he gazed absent-mindedly at the ground for some moments.

"Well," he said at length, "it's a big responsibility to take, and I don't know that I ought to assume it, but there doesn't seem to be anything else to do—short of giving you up."

His eyes sought Stone's and held them.

"Mr. Stone," he continued, speaking slowly, "I need not repeat that I'm in a position to cause your arrest at any moment, and to give the most damaging testimony against you. I don't want to do it, because of what I believe in regard to your condition, but you may be sure that I'll do it at the drop of the hat if anything happens to Mr. Crawford or if you make any other attempt on his life. Now, remembering that, will you give me your solemn promise—will you swear, in fact—that you'll have no other crime against you, and that when you reach New York you'll do as I say?"

The bronzed miner hesitated for some time, then held out his hand, which Floyd took.

"I swear to you, Charlie," he said, "that I won't start anything myself, if that's what you want. Of course, if Crawford tries anything on me I'll have to defend myself. You couldn't expect me to take it without lifting a finger."

"Certainly not," the young doctor agreed. "Mind you, though, you've got to refrain from anything hostile, unless you actually catch him in an attempt on you—which is out of the question, as he would be incapable of doing such a thing."

"Incapable your grandmother!" was the scornful response. "You don't know Win Crawford as well as I do. I've given you my word, though. Now what else do you want?"

"I want you to remember what will happen to you if you fail to keep this oath. Will you?"

"I ain't likely to forget. Is that all? What was it you wanted me to do in New York?"

"To go to see some one who can help you, if any one can."

"You mean a doctor?"

"Yes, a great one—the head of one of the biggest hospitals in the city."

"Look here!" Stone burst out angrily. "Are you trying to have me sent to an asylum?"

"Not at all," Floyd hastened to say in a soothing tone. "Doctor Follansbee isn't very keen on asylums, except as a last resort. He's a famous specialist in nervous and mental diseases, but his chief aim is always to keep people out of asylums, if possible; in other words, to cure them without interfering with their liberty or branding them as insane. I desire you to go to him—in fact, I must insist upon your doing so, if I'm to shield you from the consequences of this morning's act. If, as I suspect, your mind is slightly affected in this one respect, he may be able to help you very easily, and if he does, you'll never cease to be grateful to him. If, on the other hand, he finds you perfectly sane, there will be nothing more to be said, and I'll continue to keep silence unless you make some further attempt on Mr. Crawford. You need not fear to consult Doctor Follansbee. As I say, he'll never think of sending a man like you to an asylum, and, as people go to him for all sorts of nervous troubles as well as for operations, no one outside will draw any conclusions if your visit to him is known. Will you promise to call on him as soon as you reach New York?"

"I suppose so," Stone agreed reluctantly. "It's mighty hard lines to be ordered about like this, and sent to one of those confounded alienist fellows, but you've got the whip hand just now, Charlie, and it's up to me to take my medicine. Where will I find the wonderful Follansbee?"

Doctor Floyd took a letter from his pocket, removed the envelope, and scribbled the name and address on the back. When he handed it to Stone the latter read:

"Doctor Stephen Follansbee, St. Swithin's Hospital, Amsterdam Avenue, New York City."

"There you are," Floyd said. "I know you don't want to do this, Mr. Stone, and that it's all you can stand to have me make this condition, but I'm afraid you'll have to put up with it. It's that—or the other, and I imagine you would find a trial and conviction for attempted murder a little more irksome than either of the things I have asked you to do."

"I guess that's right," admitted the miner. "You're a good fellow, Charlie, and I know you mean well. You've rubbed it in pretty thoroughly, and there's a lot you don't understand; but I reckon I'm lucky at that. I'll keep my hands off Win Crawford until I've the chance to see this Follansbee person. After that—well, we'll see what we shall see."

"That's all I can ask at present," Floyd returned, "and you can rely on Doctor Follansbee's word. He's a queer-looking individual, and very eccentric. You needn't be surprised if he seems to agree with everything you say about Mr. Craw-ford. His methods are all his own, and they seem very peculiar at times, but he gets results in the most wonderful way. I know, because I studied under him in medical school. He's far from a beauty, and has a manner which antagonizes a good many, but he's too big to care about that. Here comes Mr. Crawford, though. Remember your promise, and don't try any tricks!"

CHAPTER III.

AN UNFORTUNATE LETTER.

The young physician halted at a little distance and watched the meeting between the two partners.

Crawford had been trudging along with head bent, as if brooding over the loss of his faithful animal and the mystery of that unexpected shot, but when he looked up at length and saw Stone, he hastened his steps and called after him.

His genial greeting was borne to Floyd's ears.

"Hello, Jimmy!" Crawford shouted. "How's the boy this morning?"

There was nothing for Stone to do but to halt and turn. He nodded curtly, however, and when they walked on together, it was evident that Crawford was doing all the talking.

"That's a queer deal," thought Floyd, with a puzzled, apprehensive look on his face. "If Stone isn't touched in the head, I'll miss my guess, but I can't imagine what the cause of it is. They've been pals for years, and have gone through thick and thin together. Their friendship has been the talk of this mining country for I don't know how long, and Crawford seems to be as fond of his partner as ever, in spite of all the rebuffs he has given him lately. I'm afraid I've made a big mistake and been altogether too easy on Stone. I'd never forgive myself if anything happened to Crawford, but it didn't seem right to make the other suffer for that insane act."

He went about his duties in an absent-minded way, however, and had done a great deal of thinking before he encountered Crawford that afternoon, as he was making his rounds. The two men greeted each other cordially, and after Floyd had looked about to see that they were unobserved he said quickly:

"I'll walk along for a short distance with you, if I may, Mr. Crawford. I find myself in a very difficult position, and what I've decided to say seems like a very serious breach of confidence. I feel that I must say it, though, because otherwise the responsibility would be too heavy for me to bear."

Crawford looked at him keenly.

"Is it about Jimmy Stone?" he asked.

"How did you guess?" was the surprised query.

"Oh, I'm not blind, Charlie, and I can put two and two together. Jimmy hasn't been himself for months, and I know others have noticed it. I saw him talking with you this morning. Have you any idea what is the matter with him?"

The young physician tapped his forehead significantly.

"I'm afraid it's—a little of that," he answered reluctantly.

"You do? I feared something of the sort, but I hoped I was mistaken. What a pity! Jimmy has always been one of the finest and whitest men that ever stepped the earth, and a friend worth having. I've worried and worried over him lately, and tried to recall anything I had said or done that might have turned him against me. I haven't been able to think of a thing that any man in his sound sense would resent to such an extent, and I've been obliged to come to the conclusion that he was not altogether responsible. Do you think anything can be done for him? We've both got plenty of money now, and I'm ready and willing— —"

"I'm sure you are, Mr. Crawford," Floyd assured him, "and I hope Mr. Stone can be helped. In fact, I'm almost sure he can be. He's absolutely normal in every other way, and this change is so recent that the trouble can't be very deep-seated. He has promised me that he will consult a famous alienist in New York."

"He has?"

Crawford gave a start as he put the question.

"Then you've actually talked with him about it?" he went on wonderingly. "Has he sought your advice?"

"Hardly," was the reply. "I butted in, and, of course, he was up in arms in a moment. Nobody likes to be called crazy—least of all a crazy man. It had to be done, though. If I tell you something, will you give me your word not to use it in any way against Mr. Stone?"

"Of course. I'd protect Jimmy's life at the risk of my own any day."

"I haven't a doubt of it, but this is asking a great deal of you. Mr. Crawford, it was—it was your partner who fired that shot at you this morning."

Crawford gave the young doctor a long, searching look, and then said quietly:

"That isn't exactly news to me, Charlie. I guessed as much."

"You did? And yet you could greet him as you did?"

"Why not? It was not the Jimmy Stone I've known for twenty years or more who did it. It was this surly, glowering chap who has stepped into his shoes. I don't bear any ill will—I can't. I've been looking for something of the sort, and of course I've tried to protect myself and shall continue to do so. I have no intention of having him confined, though, and you must promise me that you won't take any such steps. There's no danger to any one else, and if I choose to run the risk it's my own business."

"I knew that would be your attitude," Floyd told him, "and I allowed myself to promise Mr. Stone that on certain conditions I would not play the part of informer."

"You accused him of it, then?"

"Yes. I witnessed the whole thing, and told him I had done so. I used my knowledge to extract a couple of promises from him, but since then I've been wondering if I did right. I've worried a lot about the possible consequences to you, and finally I made up my mind that I'd simply have to warn you. Strictly speaking, I didn't give my word to say nothing to you. I simply agreed not to inform the authorities; but of course Stone did not dream that I would tell you, and I feel like a sneak in doing so. I couldn't bear to let you remain in ignorance, however, for if I had, I would have felt that I was indirectly responsible if anything happened to you."

Crawford nodded slowly and gripped the young physician's shoulder.

"I understand, Charlie," he said. "It was a knotty problem, but you've solved it the best you knew how, and I thank you for your warning, although it wasn't necessary. What were the promises Jimmy gave you?"

"I made him swear that he would make no further attempt on you unless in self-defense. Nothing can persuade him, you know, that you aren't gunning for him, but I knew if he kept that promise nothing would happen. It was a long chance to take with a man in his mental condition, I suppose, but I couldn't bear the thought of giving him up to justice."

Crawford nodded understandingly.

"Nor can I," he said. "I hope he'll keep the promise, knowing the light in which your testimony would place him if he didn't, but I don't intend to change my plans in the least. I'll keep an eye on him as best I can, but we'll travel together unless he refuses. If he finishes me—well, so be it. The responsibility will be mine, not yours. But what about the other promise? Was it that he should seek the advice of a specialist in New York?"

"Yes. I gave him the name of Doctor Stephen Follansbee, the famous head of St. Swithin's Hospital. Doctor Follansbee is at the top of his profession in New York, and has a great reputation for handling such cases in an unusual way without resorting to the customary confinement of the patient."

"Good! Nothing could be better! If Jimmy goes to him, we'll hope that all will come out right, and that I'll soon have my old partner back. I thank you from the bottom of my heart, Charlie, but we'd better separate now. If Jimmy should happen to see us together, or hear that we had been, he might smell a rat and make things decidedly unpleasant for you."

They shook hands again and separated, but Doctor Floyd felt that he had one more duty to perform that day. When he returned to the rough little shack which he occupied, his first act after supper was to sit down and write a rather lengthy letter. It was addressed to his former professor, Doctor Follansbee, and in it he gave the celebrated alienist a history of James Stone's case, so far as he knew it. He wished Follansbee to receive the letter before Stone's arrival, and to have something else to go on besides the man's own statements.

Incidentally, knowing that Follansbee's charges were very high, he thought best to mention the facts concerning the recent sale of the mine. He informed the specialist that Stone and Crawford had been equal partners in the Condor, and that the share of each was reputed to be five hundred thousand dollars. For no particular reason, he added that so far as was known Stone and Crawford were alone in the world, and that the general understanding was that each had drawn a will in favor of the other before the estrangement had come about.

Young Floyd was nothing if not thorough, but had he known the consequences which would follow the writing of that letter he would have cut off his right hand rather than send it.

CHAPTER IV.
CRAWFORD IS TROUBLED.

The boat deck of the *Cortez* was of wide expanse, shaded by gleaming canvas.

The South American liner had just passed Sandy Hook, bound inward, and was making its stately way toward New York harbor. It was late in the evening, and in a couple of deck chairs two figures were seated. The men were chatting together quietly. The taller of the two, clean-shaven and keen-faced, was puffing contentedly on a fragrant Havana.

They were Nick Carter, the distinguished New York detective, and his leading assistant, Chick Carter, who were returning from a couple of weeks' holiday spent in Jamaica. The *Cortez* had touched at Kingston on its way north from South American ports, and it was there that the detective and his assistant had come on board.

"Evidently we won't be home until to-morrow morning," Chick Carter said quietly. "It will be too late for disembarking to-night. Of course we could get a special dispensation, if necessary, but I don't believe in pulling wires unless there's need for it. All the same, I'll be glad to get back into harness again."

Chick grinned in the darkness. He had enjoyed their short stay in beautiful Jamaica, but he had noted that his chief had chafed at the idleness, especially during the last few days.

"Let's hope there's something waiting for us that will let us sit up and take notice," he said. "I feel fit to tackle anything."

They were both in evening dress and awaiting the sound of the dinner gong, which soon called them to the saloon.

There were over fifty first-class passengers on board, and at the detective's table were two men who had interested him. They sat side by side opposite to him, and their broad shoulders and tanned features told plainly that they were men who had spent the greater part of their years out of doors in some hot country.

Their manners and dress were curiously alike, but their faces differed greatly. The man who sat on the right, and who Nick had found out was Winthrop Crawford, had an open, kindly countenance. The trim gray beard did not quite hide the friendly lines about the mouth; and the eyes, although set in a network of wrinkles—such as one always notices on the faces of those who have peered long over sun-drenched stretches of plain or mountain—were wide and blue and looked out on the world in a genial fashion.

His companion, however, was almost the opposite, so far as looks were concerned. There was nothing repellent about his features, to be sure, but his expression was far from agreeable. His eyes were hard and suspicious, his lips usually wore either a snarl or a sneer, and his brows were drawn together with a surly frown most of the time.

It was the head steward who had told Nick the names of the two men, and had also added the information that they had been until recently joint owners of a big silver mine in South America.

The second man, James Stone, was the older of the two, and it was his peculiar manner that had interested the detective first of all. During the four or five days since Carter and his assistant had boarded the *Cortez*, they had never heard Stone say more than half a dozen words at a time to any one, even to his companion, Crawford. At the table Nick noted that Crawford often tried to engage his partner in conversation, but his efforts were always doomed to failure. Moreover, the detective had observed the perplexed, anxious look which had come into Crawford's eyes many times after these rebuffs.

The two mining men were in their places when Carter and Chick dropped into their seats. Once or twice in the course of the meal the detective caught Crawford glancing across at him with a look of interest, and wondered what it meant. He was not surprised, therefore, when, after the meal was over and he had entered the smoking room, he heard a voice at his elbow, and, turning round, saw the bearded face of Winthrop Crawford at his side.

"I hope you'll excuse me, Mr. Carter," the man said in a deep, melodious voice, "but I've just heard from the steward who you are, and I'd like to make your acquaintance."

As a judge of character Nick Carter had no superior, and he saw that the man in front of him was of the sterling, honest type; therefore, he had no hesitation in holding out his hand.

"It's only another case of diamond cut diamond, Mr. Crawford," he answered, with a smile, "for I must also plead guilty to having made inquiries about you."

Crawford pulled out a cigar case, and Nick accepted the "weed," after which they strolled across the big room and seated themselves on a comfortable settee.

"I'm returning to New York after an absence of a quarter of a century," Crawford explained, "and I don't believe I know a single soul there."

"You are taking a well-earned vacation, I suppose?" the detective remarked.

"Something of the sort," was the answer. "As a matter of fact, I have no occupation now, since my partner and I have sold out our mining interests in South America. I have nothing definite in view, but I'm sure I shan't be content to remain idle for long."

He leaned back and puffed at his cigar.

"I've had a pretty tough time of it," he went on. "The usual experience of those who knock about the world seeking their fortunes; but I think I can safely say that

I'm secure now for the rest of my life—unless I make a fool of myself."

"I'm very glad to hear of it," Nick declared heartily. "I understood that you and Mr. Stone had been fortunate."

Crawford nodded his head, but a shadow passed over his face.

"It isn't necessary to go into details, Mr. Carter," he replied, "but your informant was quite correct. Stone and I discovered and developed the Condor Mine in Brazil. We worked it ourselves for over a year, and then decided to sell out and come back home. It netted us about half a million apiece. That's very little, of course, as you count wealth up here, but it's enough for us to live on in comfort for the rest of our lives. We have no one dependent on us—unfortunately."

"I'm sure you deserve it all," the detective told him warmly.

Crawford's eyes grew misty with a host of memories of hard days and lean ones—days when the nearest approach to a meal had been another notch in the belt and the hope of something more substantial on the morrow.

"Yes," he said thoughtfully, "I've earned it; and that brings me to something I wanted to say. I'm a little afraid of your New York, Mr. Carter. I know much more about prospecting than I do about finance. As I've told you, there's nothing to occupy my mind, and I suppose I'll soon be looking about for investments. If I'm not very careful, I'm likely to fall among thieves."

He leaned across and placed his hand on Nick's arm.

"Even in South America we hear of Nick Carter," he said, with a quiet nod of his grizzled head, "and I count it a very fortunate chance that I should have run across you here on this vessel. I have engaged rooms at the Hotel Windermere, and I'll be very glad if you'll give me your address. I should like to have some one to go to for advice if I find that the sharks begin to gather."

Then, as the detective remained silent, Crawford went on:

"It must be a strictly business undertaking, you understand. If I'm doubtful about any concern or individual, I would like to call on you and have you give me a report. I should expect you to make the usual charge for such work—in fact, I would be willing to pay more than that, because, as a friendless man who doesn't understand the game, I would profit more than usual by such invaluable assistance."

There was something curiously winning about Crawford's voice, and the man appealed strongly to Nick. The sort of assistance he asked for was hardly in the detective's line, but the simple, direct appeal gained the day.

"Very well," he said, taking out his case and handing a card to Crawford. "Let's hope for your sake that you won't have any very urgent need of me, but here's my address, and you can ring me up at any time. I shall be very glad to do anything I can."

Crawford had just placed the card in his pocket when the door of the smoking room opened and James Stone appeared. There was a little bar at one end of the room, and it was toward this that Crawford's partner was headed. Stone's eyes traveled across to Crawford, and the latter made a move as though to rise to his feet, but his partner turned his head away quickly and went on his way. There was more than a suggestion of surliness, if not of enmity, in the way he ignored Crawford, and the latter leaned back again with an involuntary sigh.

Nick caught his eye.

"I can't make it out," Crawford said at last, the troubled expression deepening on his face. "I suppose you've noted that Stone and I hardly exchange a word."

CHAPTER V.

ANOTHER MURDEROUS ATTACK.

"I must admit that I have noticed it," Nick returned, "and it struck me as being rather curious, under the circumstances."

"It beats me," Crawford declared, glancing down at the bar, where the broad-shouldered figure of his old comrade was standing. "Jimmy and I have been chums for years. We've worked together and starved together, and five years ago he saved my life at the risk of his own. He dived into a flooded river, and it was touch and go whether he brought me out or not."

The deep voice shook for a moment. "It's beyond me," he continued. "For the last few months he's been a changed man. I can hardly get a word out of him, and many times I've caught him looking at me as though I were his bitterest enemy."

There was no doubting the sincerity of Crawford's emotions. His tanned face twitched, and his hard, work-worn hands were clasped in a tight grip as they rested on his knees.

"Something has gone wrong," he concluded, "but what it is Heaven only knows. Would you believe me if I told you that he— —"

The detective waited curiously, but Crawford did not complete the sentence, and a little silence fell between the two.

As Stone had tossed off his drink, he passed them once more. When he reached the door, however, he halted for a moment, then, swinging around on his heel, beckoned to Crawford. It was almost a gasp of relief that broke from the latter's lips as he rose.

"Hello!" he murmured. "He wants to speak to me, does he? Excuse me, Mr. Carter."

The eager way in which he hurried toward his partner revealed to the detective how anxious he was to make friends again.

The two figures passed out through the doorway, and Nick mechanically picked up a magazine from a neighboring table. Half an hour passed; then, leaving the smoking room, the detective went off in search of Chick. His young assistant was not to be seen, and presently Carter returned to the boat deck, found a quiet gap between two suspended boats, and, leaning on the rail, watched the distant lights along the coast.

Perhaps fifteen minutes later the detective heard a quick, muffled cry, followed by the creak of a boat as some heavy object swung against it. He straightened up and listened. A moment later a half-choked voice came to him:

"Jim! Jim! Good heavens! Are you trying to murder me?"

Nick recognized the voice as that of Crawford's, and, with a swift bound, he leaped out of the dark gap between the boats in which he had stood concealed.

Sprinting forward along the deserted deck, he followed the direction of the sound, and in another gap he saw standing out against the background of the sea two struggling figures. They were locked in each other's arms, and one of them was swaying out over the rail at a perilous angle. The detective saw that the figure of the man bending over the rail was that of Crawford, and above him, with his fingers clutched tightly around his throat, was James Stone. The former was clutching at the murderous wrists of his companion, trying to release the fierce grip, but even as Nick sighted them Stone made another vicious lunge, and Crawford's body was all but thrust out over the rail into the sea.

A swift, horrified spring carried Nick into the gap between the boats, and realizing that there was not a moment to spare, he flung himself at Stone. It was a straight-arm blow that the detective gave, with the swift, trained precision of an experienced athlete. The great detective's bunched fist landed full on the hard, dogged face of James Stone with resistless force. A strangled oath broke from the miner's lips, and he staggered back against the bow of the swinging boat, releasing Crawford as he did so.

Nick saw the unfortunate man's body sway over the rail, and with a headlong leap the detective hurled himself forward, gripping at the toppling man. He was only just in the nick of time. His fingers caught the ends of Crawford's evening coat, and for a long tense moment he hung over the rail, clutching in that way the otherwise unsupported body of the miner. It was well for Crawford that the muscles of those two arms were of a man much beyond the average strength. Carter felt as though his arms were being pulled out of their sockets, but presently he gathered himself for an extra effort, and slowly and carefully pulled the swaying man upward until Crawford was able to grasp the rail in his hands. A moment later, Nick had shifted his grasp until his palms were under the man's shoulders, and then with a tug Crawford was lifted over the rail and deposited safely on the deck.

The perspiration was pouring from the detective's face, and his breath was coming and going in great, choking pants, for Crawford was a heavy man and the bodily effort had been a tremendous one. The miner clung to the rail for a few moments, steadying himself there. Through the gloom Nick could see the bearded face and the blue eyes fixed on his own. At that instant, a quick, shuffling footfall came to the detective's ears, and he turned quickly around in time to see the figure of Stone gliding like a black shadow along the pale, canvas-covered side of the suspended boat.

"Oh, no, you don't, you confounded rascal!" Nick broke out, as he started to follow the man.

But before he could do so, Crawford reeled, stepped toward him, and clutched him by the arm.

"It's—it's you, Carter?" the miner breathed.

"Yes. Let me go, though. I don't want that scoundrel to get away."

Crawford's fingers tightened their hold on his sleeve.

"Don't follow him! Let him go—for my sake!" he pleaded.

Nick paused and peered with surprise into the man's face.

"I suppose you know what you're saying?" the detective asked, in a strange voice.

"Perfectly."

"But that fellow tried to murder you."

"I know that only too well."

"And you mean to say you're not going to lodge a complaint against him or do anything in the matter?"

The bearded face shone in the dusk.

"That man will never be accused by me," Crawford said positively. "Don't you recognize him?"

The detective shrugged his shoulders.

"Yes, I recognize him, all right," he said. "It was Stone, your partner, and also—if I had not come on the scene just when I did—your murderer."

Crawford came closer to Carter and thrust his arm through that of the detective.

"That may be," he said, "but I can't forget that he's also the man who once saved my life, who has shared his last crust with me again and again."

Then, as an exclamation of impatience broke from Nick's lips, the miner went on:

"Oh, yes, I know that you think me a fool. You will think me even a greater when I tell you that this is not the first time. He has tried to do the same thing on this very voyage—to say nothing of an attempt before we left South America."

CHAPTER VI.

THE LOVE OF COMRADES.

"Good heavens!" Nick Carter broke out. "Do you actually mean to tell me that he has attacked you before?"

"I do," the deep voice replied. "He tried to shoot me from ambush a week or so before we left Brazil, and just prior to our arrival at Kingston he made another attempt. He was not nearly so successful that time, though. I managed to over-power him."

They were pacing along the dark deck now, and Nick heard the man by his side draw a deep breath.

"Something has gone wrong with Jimmy Stone," he said quietly. "You don't know him as I do, Carter. Up to a short six months ago he was like a brother to me. Man, I tell you that Jim Stone is the only person in the world that I—I care two straws about. You know what it means to men who have lived and starved together."

The rich voice stopped, and Nick caught something that was suspiciously like a suppressed sob. Involuntarily he paused, and Crawford halted for a moment, his shoulders shaking.

A strong man's grief is a terrible thing to witness, and the detective felt himself tongue-tied.

"My friend—my old comrade!" Crawford went on huskily. "Trying to murder me! By Heaven, Carter, it almost breaks my heart!"

He swung around suddenly and caught Nick by the arm again.

"I want you to keep this thing a secret," he said earnestly. "Jim isn't account-able for this mood that has been on him for the last few months—he isn't account-able for his actions. I had feared for some time that there was a little trouble with his brain, and my suspicions were confirmed before we left South America."

He then went on to tell in detail of Stone's attempt to shoot him, as revealed by the young physician; of the latter's opinion of Stone's sanity—or, rather, insan-ity—and finally of the promise Floyd had wrung from the misguided man.

He told the detective that Stone had reluctantly agreed to consult a famous specialist, but only because he had felt compelled to do so in order to stop Floyd's mouth. Unfortunately, however, he had forgotten the specialist's name and that of the hospital of which he was the head.

Had Nick learned those important facts, there might have been a different story to tell.

"You will help me shield him, won't you, Carter?" Crawford begged. "I suppose I haven't any right to ask it, but, after all, it's my funeral and not yours. That's what I told Floyd. He couldn't rest until he had warned me, but it did not seem right for me to change my plans in any way. Jim is my oldest and best friend—my only close friend, in fact—and I couldn't bear to cut adrift from him. Besides, I've been hoping all the time that he'd come out from under this cloud; that I'd find some way of reaching his heart and making it all right again. I have tried time after time, but always failed. He thinks I'm his enemy, and attributes to me all the evil suspicions that are bred in his poor diseased brain. It seems hopeless, unless he can get some help, but whatever happens I'm going to stick to him. There's so little the matter with him, you see, and I know that the man himself is one of the finest. He would never dream of hurting any one if he were in his right mind, least of all me."

"I have no doubt you are right about that," the detective agreed, "and that you're the only one who is in any danger from him; nevertheless, I can't help thinking that your affection, highly commendable as it is, has caused you to take a very foolish risk. You say yourself that you haven't been able to do him any good, and certainly he doesn't take any pleasure in your society, to say the least. It was very unwise of you to have traveled all this distance with him, and to have occupied an adjoining stateroom. It has simply put temptation in his way. You don't want to make him a murderer, do you, aside from the question of your own safety?"

"No, no! Heaven knows I don't!"

"Then you ought by all means to keep out of his way," Nick advised gravely. "You say that this Doctor Floyd extracted a promise from him that he would do nothing more against you until he had seen this specialist, but you admit that he has broken that promise not less than twice during the voyage. Plainly there's no reliance to be placed in him, as there never is in the case of any one who is mentally affected even in the slightest degree."

"I know," admitted Crawford. "Jimmy doesn't think he has broken his promise, though. He made a condition that he should do nothing unless I provoked it or he was obliged to act in self-defense. I'm sure he thinks he has adhered to that condition. Both times when he has pounced on me he snarled, 'You would, would you?' or something like that, as if I had made some move to attack him."

"That's just it," commented the detective. "He's obviously unbalanced, and imagines all sorts of things. Under the circumstances, therefore, you can do him no possible good, and may lose your life at any moment."

The miner shook his head.

"I realize that what you say is all true," he admitted, "but I'm afraid I'm a fatalist, Mr. Carter. I simply can't turn my back on Jimmy. I feel that I must stick by him for the sake of old times, and, besides, it seems like cowardice to do anything else. I've never been a coward, and I don't want to begin now. Anyway, I have engaged rooms for both of us at the Windermere, connecting rooms. I'd feel like a selfish sneak if I made any change. I don't want Jimmy to have my blood on his head, or the blood of any one, and I hope and pray it won't come to that; but the bonds between us are too strong to be broken by me. You see how it is, Mr. Carter, and that it's hopeless to argue with me. Are you willing to let me go my way in this, and to promise me that you'll not take any action whatever?"

The anxiety in his voice indicated how keenly Crawford felt the situation. On the one hand, the man's amazing obstinacy made Nick very impatient, but on the other, he felt a strange admiration for Crawford's unfaltering loyalty. He thrust out his hand in the darkness, and the palms of the two men met.

"All right, Crawford," he said, and his voice was deep and vibrating. "I think you're making a mistake, but it's the kind of mistake one can't help honoring you for. I look upon you as one of the bravest men I have ever met, and you may be sure that I will keep your secret."

Crawford wrung the outstretched hand.

"I thank you with all my heart," he said, "and I—I won't forget that you saved my life. Some day I hope to be able to repay you. In any event, we'll meet again in New York."

But neither he nor Nick dreamed of the curious circumstances that were to draw them together again in the great city.

CHAPTER VII.

FOLLANSBEE HITS THE NAIL.

It was little after eleven o'clock in the morning when a broad-shouldered man turned into Amsterdam Avenue and began to move slowly along the pavement, glancing now and then at the houses as he passed. His tanned face suggested that he was a man from a warmer land, and the stubborn chin and hard, sour look about the eyes were mute tokens of the surly temper that ruled the stranger. He was wearing a soft hat with a wide brim, and he had tilted it forward to shade his eyes from the sun. Once he took a slip of paper from his pocket and studied it for a moment. Evidently he was looking for an address.

Presently he caught sight of what he sought—the big bulk of St. Swithin's Hospital, which occupied an entire block. He quickened his pace and approached the great building. In the reception room, however, a disappointment awaited him. When he asked for Doctor Stephen Follansbee, he was told that that distinguished individual had not yet arrived at the hospital that day. But after some argument he obtained Follansbee's private address, which proved to be also on Amsterdam Avenue and not more than half a dozen blocks away.

The stranger retraced his steps, therefore, and sought the new number. He soon found it over the door of a house that was one of a row of solid but by no means impressive residences.

A maid admitted him and asked if he had an appointment with the doctor. When informed that he had not, she invited him into the empty reception room and told him Doctor Follansbee was busy, but that he would be free in a few minutes. The visitor seated himself, picked up a magazine, and began mechanically glancing it over. After ten or fifteen minutes, the folding doors at the rear of the reception room were opened and a patient emerged. Over the latter's shoulder the waiting man caught a glimpse of a stern, repellent figure in the doorway.

The caller rose expectantly, but before he had a chance to step forward or utter a word he was greeted in an unexpected, almost uncanny, fashion.

"Come in, Mr. Stone!" were the words which came from the man in the doorway.

With a start, James Stone grasped his hat and stepped forward. He could not imagine by what black art the master of the house knew his name, and he eyed his host apprehensively as he passed him and entered the room beyond.

He was doubtless face to face with the famous Doctor Stephen Follansbee, but it was hard, indeed, to believe it. The man before him could not have been more than five feet high. His head was as bare as a billiard ball and curiously elongated in shape. The vulturelike face, the almost fringeless eyelids, and the long, thin, hawklike nose held him mute.

Into the black, beady eyes there flickered a sudden mirth, and the thin lips twisted into what was the ghost of a smile.

"It's all right, Stone!" the extraordinary individual declared. "You have come to the right place. You may not think it, but I'm Doctor Follansbee."

Was it possible? The man looked like some sinister bird of prey, and yet he was at the head of a celebrated hospital and enjoyed the most enviable reputation as an authority whose fame was countrywide.

In response to a gesture from Follansbee the visitor dropped into a chair close beside a small desk that stood by a window. The specialist crossed the room with quick, birdlike steps and took his seat behind the desk. In the momentary pause that followed, the two men eyed each other, but what their thoughts were remained their respective secrets. At least, Stone could not read the physician's.

"You expected to see some one very different, I suppose?" Follansbee remarked, with a mocking smile. "A big, well-groomed figurehead with an impressive manner and a carefully trimmed Vandyke beard? Confess, now."

Stone relaxed and laughed. It was a short, grating laugh, and the physician's eyes dilated slightly as he heard it.

It was hardly the laugh of a sane person, and as Follansbee leaned forward he noted that the pupils of Stone's eyes were fixed and round, a sign which the initiated always searches for in mental cases.

"That's about it," the visitor admitted, in his harsh voice. "The—the young man who spoke to me about you told me that you were the head of a big hospital, and I've just been there."

Follansbee nodded.

"I understand," he said. "I can assure you that your friend was quite correct, as you've doubtless found out for yourself, if you've been at St. Swithin's. I've never been called handsome, but I haven't found that a drawback, and I suspect that you didn't come to see me for my looks. Did you have a pleasant voyage on the *Cortez*?"

Stone looked at him in open-mouthed amazement.

"What do you know about me?" he demanded. "You nearly floored me by calling me by my name, and now you— —"

"Oh, that isn't all I know about you," Follansbee assured him maliciously. "I can tell you all about the Condor Mine and of your partner, Winthrop Crawford—or shall we call him your ex-partner? I know that you and he recently sold the Condor for a million, and that you have both come back to your old stamping ground after an absence of a quarter of a century or so. I know several other things, too, but we won't speak of them just yet."

Stone bit his lip and paled a little under his tan.

"Well, I'll be hanged!" he muttered. "I suppose Floyd must have written to you about me. How in thunder you knew me, though, when I came in, is more than I can understand."

"Who may 'Floyd' be?" queried Follansbee, as if he had never heard the name before.

His visitor looked at him in bewilderment, but again failed to read that baffling countenance.

"Why, he's the young American doctor down in Brazil who advised me to come to you," he explained wonderingly. "He said he had studied under you in medical school."

"Indeed! That's very interesting," murmured the specialist. "Hundreds of young men have studied under me, however. I suppose I might say thousands. It is gratifying to be remembered by one of them, of course, but I cannot be expected——"

"Then how in the world——"

"Let's not waste time over things out of our immediate concern," Follansbee interrupted. "Please remember that my time is valuable, very valuable. You seem to be slow in getting to the point. I'll help you out. I happen to know the nature of your errand, but am also perfectly well aware that your heart isn't in it. Your real desires are of a very different sort. Isn't that so?"

James Stone looked alarmed, as well he might. His conscience was by no means clear, and the conversation seemed to be getting on decidedly dangerous ground.

"I—I don't know what you're talking about," he faltered, moistening his lips. "Doctor Floyd had a fool notion that I was going crazy, or something like that. I naturally didn't take very kindly to the idea, but I was more or less under obligations to him, and he was so insistent that I promised to look you up. He said you would help me. Of course, I don't think I need any help—of that sort—but I'm a man of my word, and that's why I'm here."

"Very commendable!" murmured the head of St. Swithin's. "Doctor Boyd, or whatever his name is, was quite right. I can help you, in more ways than one, and I perceive that what you really want is to be rid of your former partner, Winthrop Crawford. Have I hit the nail on the head?"

A meaning smile crossed the sinister face, and Follansbee leaned back in his chair, the glance from his hard little eyes playing over his caller's face.

CHAPTER VIII.

"NAME YOUR PRICE."

James Stone looked as if the ground had suddenly caved from under his feet. His big body stiffened, his hands clutched his hat, and his startled eyes were riveted on Follansbee's countenance. He moistened his dry lips again and attempted to speak, but it ended only in a swallow, as evidenced by the movement in his throat.

The great specialist seemed to enjoy the sensation he had made.

"You know, Mr. Stone," he went on, "that we doctors have a way, sometimes, of locating a patient's trouble by feeling him over until we find a tender spot. When he winces, we know we've struck it, and we draw our own conclusions. It's obvious that I've found your tender spot; therefore, there isn't any use in your beating about the bush. I know that you desire to eliminate Crawford. I might use a stronger expression, but I'll spare your feelings to that extent. Out with it, now, man! You have a lot of poison bottled up in your system. Let it come out. If there's anything wrong with you mentally, as your friend in Brazil seems to have thought, I'll find it out and make due allowances. On the other hand, if you're sane, you need be no more afraid of confiding in me. I'm not a policeman, you know—or a judge. Remember, too, that I have said I could help you."

It was not so much his words, but the manner in which he uttered them that gave James Stone a certain confidence.

Follansbee was as far removed as possible from the type of the kindly, tolerant, helpful physician. On the contrary, everything said, every glance he cast—the whole man, in fact—would have been highly distasteful to the average person. It was that very thing, however, that tended to draw Stone out and to make him reveal the murderous impulses which controlled him.

It seemed incredible, but he had a feeling that he had nothing to fear from the famous Doctor Follansbee; in fact, that the latter was a possible ally. And in support of that startling belief, certain words of young Floyd's came to him.

Floyd had said that Follansbee was very eccentric, had ways of doing things that were all his own, and was in the habit of seeming to sympathize with those who came to him, no matter what they might say or do.

The young physician had evidently been a firm believer in the man who had once been his professor, but Stone found himself wondering if Follansbee was what he had seemed to Floyd. He doubted it, and decided he had found a kindred spirit. Follansbee's mask seemed to be slipping off.

Emboldened by this, the miner dropped his great hands on his knees and leaned forward, flinging a quick glance about him as he did so.

"Are you sure we'll not be heard here?" he asked, cunning returning to his eyes.

"Perfectly," was the answer. "My servants are well trained, and these walls are much thicker than those they put into the houses they build nowadays. You can talk openly and freely, Stone, and your secrets will be guarded."

Stone nodded, and the glitter in his eyes became more pronounced.

"You are right, Doctor Follansbee," he said. "I can't figure out how you know, but I want to get rid of Win Crawford. I—I want to get rid of him before he gets rid of me."

His heavy face was wrinkled into a mask of cunning—the foolish, vacant cunning of the insane.

"He thinks he's clever," Stone went on; "thinks I don't know what he's going to do. But I'm as cute as he is, and I've tumbled to him."

Follansbee had folded his long, flexible fingers and was leaning his shoulders on the arms of his chair. His evil-looking eyes were slowly taking on a mocking twinkle as they looked at the features of the man in front of him.

The skilled specialist had no further doubt about the matter. At that moment he knew to a certainty that James Stone was mad, and that his was the most dangerous form of insanity, for it centered only on one object.

Outwardly and in his everyday life, Stone might move and conduct himself as an ordinary individual, but lurking always in his diseased brain was one wild and terrible fancy—an insane fear and hatred of the man who in the brighter, if less prosperous, past he had once risked his life to save.

It remained to be seen, however, in what Follansbee's treatment of the case would consist.

"So you think that your partner is going to kill you, do you?" the specialist asked.

"I don't think—I know!" the husky voice returned. "All this is only a game of his. He has brought me to New York because he was afraid to do it in Brazil. I have too many friends there, but he'll find I'm too much for him. Ha, ha! He'll find out!"

The laugh was so ugly and hollow, and the man so obviously getting more and more excited that Follansbee decided to stave off a further outburst.

"That's all right," he said soothingly. "I'm sure you will be able to look after yourself."

"I'm going to do more than that," Stone announced malignantly. "I'm going to kill him before he has a chance to kill me."

It was clear that he had thrown off all fear of Follansbee, either under the influence of his own misguided desires or his belief that the head of St. Swithin's was not what he seemed to the world.

With a quick movement he rose to his feet, and, leaning over the desk, looked down into the physician's eyes with a face that worked convulsively.

"And you've got to help me!" he added. "I've tried three times to do it, twice on board the *Cortez*, but luck was against me every time."

"Three times!" Follansbee repeated, in astonishment. "Then Crawford knows what you're up to?"

"Yes, he knows," Stone answered, "but that doesn't make any difference. He's a fool, and he thinks he's got to stick by me to wait his own chance. He and I are staying at the same hotel in connecting rooms. We breakfasted at the same table this morning, and I had hard work to get away from him."

"That's queer," the specialist remarked thoughtfully. "He must be a fool!"

His surprise was genuine. He was not capable of fathoming the true cause of Crawford's devotion to his old comrade—could not understand that Stone's partner had forgiven and deliberately left his life in jeopardy for the sake of other days.

And in James Stone's distorted brain there was no more idea of the truth. He stabbed at the desk with one thick finger.

"That's his cursed cunning, I tell you!" he declared. "He's waiting until he gets good and ready to strike. By Heaven, I can't sleep at night, sometimes, for thinking of it! That's why he doesn't leave me, even though I've tried three times to kill him. He's just waiting his chance, waiting his chance."

The hoarse voice was lifted until it broke.

"But his chance isn't going to come!" the demented man insisted. "He won't live to get it! You've got to help me, I tell you. Floyd sent me to you because he caught me trying to shoot Crawford out there, and thought I was crazy. You know better, though, and I know something about you. Floyd thinks you're only a great doctor, but he's a kid, and he doesn't know the world as I do. I ain't crazy, Doctor Stephen Follansbee; I ain't a fool. Maybe New York thinks you're a saint, for all I know—though I don't see how it can when it looks at that face of yours! But I know you're not. You may be the king-pin of your profession, but you're a crook as well—as big a rascal as ever walked the earth! I know something about men, and you can't fool me.

"Now, let's get down to business," he continued. "Charlie Floyd sent me here for one kind of help, but you've opened the way for another—and that's the kind I want. I ain't very good at this sort of thing, I'll admit. I've failed three times, but if you take it on, I guess you'll get your man at the first crack. If you can't I've got you wrong. I'm willing to pay well, but I don't want any backing and filling about it. So name your price and let's get busy, Doctor Stephen Follansbee, for time is on the wing."

CHAPTER IX.

A "FAIR" OFFER.

"Sit down and cool off," Doctor Follansbee advised; and under his compelling gaze his visitor subsided and sank into a chair.

The head of St. Swithin's Hospital studied Stone for some moments without showing the slightest sign of emotion as a result of the astounding proposition which had just been made to him. His long, capable, surgeon's fingers tapped against one another, and his cold, dark eyes seemed to have no more feeling in them than a couple of highly polished stones.

"You take a great deal for granted, Mr. James Stone," he remarked at last, in his thin, squeaking tones. "I might have you confined in an asylum for that, you know—or turned over to the police."

"You might, but you won't," his caller said, with a half growl. "I've taken your measure, Follansbee, and if your time is as valuable as you say, you'll stop wasting it. I asked your price, and I'm prepared to pay anything in reason to have this business taken off my hands."

The faint semblance of a smile twisted Follansbee's thin lips.

"Rough and ready," he murmured. "A South American edition of the old 'wild and woolly' Westerner. He wants what he wants when he wants it, and he isn't bashful about asking for it."

He paused for a moment and then went on:

"Well, my genial friend, I won't abuse your confidence. Professional ethics forbid. As for your opinion of me, I care nothing for that. Perhaps I look upon it as only another evidence of mental disease."

"Will you help me or won't you?" Stone broke in.

"Most assuredly I will," was the quiet answer. "I'll help you in my own way, and if I'm to do so, you must put yourself wholly in my hands. Will you promise?"

Stone's heart sank, and he looked askance at Follansbee for a few moments. The latter's words sounded a little too professional to suit him. His belief that the physician was a rascal was rooted deep, however, and overshadowed everything else.

"I'll agree to almost anything if you'll do what I want done," he said.

"I'll do what needs to be done," was the evasive answer. "You asked my terms, though, and I must warn you that they're high. Some of the richest men in the world come to me, and I have no time to waste with those who cannot afford to pay my price. You can, if you're willing to do so."

"How much?" Stone asked, in a more subdued tone.

Follansbee's preamble sounded formidable.

"I don't expect to get you for nothing," the miner went on. "You must know of a thousand ways of—of getting rid of people—ways by which no one would be any the wiser. I'm willing to pay for that knowledge, but I'm not a millionaire, you know."

"I'm aware of that," piped Follansbee, "and shall take the fact into account. That being so, my fee will be only forty-five thousand dollars!"

James Stone started at the mention of this enormous sum.

"That is the best I can do," Doctor Follansbee went on, in his cold tones. "Remember that if I assist you to get rid of your partner, I also assist you to add his share of the proceeds from the sale of the Condor to your own." The hawklike face was very hard now, and the beady eyes glowed sternly. "You will receive at least four hundred and fifty thousand dollars after the death of Winthrop Crawford," he continued. "I'm only asking ten per cent of that amount."

His tone was calm and calculating. Stone saw the point which Follansbee had made, but he could not penetrate the latter's armor.

Follansbee had not said in so many words that he would help him to get rid of his partner. He had promised to help "in his own way." To be sure, this calculation, based on Crawford's death, seemed to commit him, but Stone found himself wondering if he were only being played with. Had the doctor merely mentioned that in order to draw him on and get his own price? Of what was the promise of help to consist? He voiced his doubts, but his words were met in the same sphinxlike way.

"I'm afraid I can't enlighten you as to that," Follansbee told him. "It isn't proper for a physician to make definite promises, and it's very unprofessional to outline methods. I have agreed to take your case for forty-five thousand dollars, and I promise to give it my best attention and the benefit of my long knowledge. That is all anybody but a quack can say. You'll have to take it or leave it. If you're so thoroughly persuaded that I'm a scoundrel, you oughtn't to hesitate."

His smile was a maddening enigma.

Under the influence of this skillful handling, the tanned face widened into a smile, and Stone nodded his head. "All right," he said. "I forgot about the money. Crawford has made his will in my favor, and if he dies without involving me I'll get his share, of course."

"That's my understanding of the situation," Follansbee agreed.

"That's right—that's right! How you got on to it, though, Heaven only knows!"

"Then you're willing to pay me the fee I demand?"

"I suppose it's worth it. Yes, I'll pay it."

"A wise decision," murmured Follansbee.

He reached out a lean hand and swung a pad of blotting paper round, then placed a pen and inkwell beside it.

"Now I want you to sit down here and write me out a check for forty-five thousand dollars. To-day is the seventeenth, and I want you to date your check the twenty-seventh. That gives me ten days, and if at the end of that time Winthrop Crawford is still troubling you, all you have to do is to go to your bank and stop payment on your check. Is that fair?"

CHAPTER X.

THE RAISED CHECK.

"I couldn't ask anything more than that," Stone admitted.

He felt sure now that Follansbee would do all he wished, despite the fact that he had been able to pin him down. He assumed that that was merely the doctor's caution and cleverness, and the offer to allow him to date the check ahead came with an unexpected sense of relief.

To be sure, Follansbee had put it with his customary vagueness. He had not said, "if at the end of that time, Crawford is still alive," but only "if he's still troubling you."

That might mean any one of a number of things, but, as was his way, Stone interpreted it as best suited him. He drew a check book from his pocket, and, pulling a chair forward, seated himself at the desk. His head was bent, and he could not see Follansbee's face. Had he been able to do so, he might have been struck by the curious look that was now in the little eyes.

When Stone had filled in the check, all except the signature, he found that the ink on the point had given out, and he stretched out his hand to dip the pen into the inkwell again. At the same moment Follansbee also reached out, apparently to push the well nearer to his visitor. Between them, in some manner the well was upset, and a small quantity of the black fluid it contained made a round patch on the top of the desk.

"Never mind!" Follansbee hastened to say, in answer to Stone's regretful exclamation. "It doesn't matter. Let it be. You can finish with this." As he spoke, he took another ink bottle from the back of the desk, removed the cork, and placed it within easy reach.

Stone mechanically dipped the pen into the new receptacle and scrawled his signature at the bottom of the check, after which he handed the slip of paper to Follansbee.

"Thanks!" the specialist said carelessly, turning the check over and blotting it on the pad. "Now give me the name of your hotel and the number of your room."

"The Hotel Windermere, room number twenty-two," was the reply.

Follansbee jotted it down on the back of a card, and then looked at his watch.

"I must be going now," he said. "I'm overdue at the hospital. I will be engaged there until six o'clock, but I'll phone you as soon after that as possible."

Stone picked up his hat and peered at the inscrutable face for a moment, as if in a last attempt to read the thoughts behind it.

"You're sure you can do it?" he asked hoarsely.

"Nothing is absolutely sure in this world, even the performance of a specialist," was the cool reply. "However"—and he tapped the check, the blank side of which was turned uppermost, with one forefinger—"there is my fee; and you may rest assured that I shall do my best to earn it."

Half insane though he was, James Stone was greatly impressed. Follansbee had not showed his hand once during the interview. At best he had only given a momentary glimpse at his cards, but there was a hint of strength, of unusual power of one kind or another behind that hard mask.

"Very well, doctor," the miner returned. "I shall expect to hear from you this evening."

He strode across the room, Follansbee following him with his short, noiseless steps. When the double doors were reached and opened, the doctor put out his hand and Stone felt a cold, dry palm thrust into his own moist, hot one.

"Until this evening," Follansbee said, with a bow that was almost courtly, despite its mocking character.

Stone passed through the reception room, and the little man closed the double doors of the office behind him.

Bending forward, Follansbee tilted his head at an angle like that of a listening bird. He remained in that position until the noise of the closing door told him that the miner had left the house; then, turning, he darted across the room toward his desk and seized upon the check. A low, disagreeable laugh broke from his lips as his eyes alighted on the face of it, for date, number, payee's name, and amount had all disappeared, and the only words that remained were the two which constituted the signature—"James Stone."

The doctor's eyes turned to the desk where the "ink" which had been used had been spilled, but the mysterious volatile liquid had already disappeared from the surface, and only a little grayish powder remained.

That, too, quickly vanished, as Follansbee blew it away.

Then, dropping into a chair in front of the desk, and in a strong, bold hand—in stern contrast to his size and quick, nervous movement—he filled in the rest of the check once more. He made it out, of course, to himself, as before, and reproduced the vanished number from memory. That was an easy matter, since he had been looking over Stone's shoulder; but this time the date put down was the twenty-fifth instead of the twenty-seventh, and the amount was not forty-five thousand dollars, but—four hundred and fifty thousand!

CHAPTER XI.

A DISTINGUISHED SCOUNDREL.

"Yes, my friend, I intend to earn my fee," the cold voice declared to the empty room. "The only difference is that the fee is somewhat larger than I've given you reason to believe."

Leaning back in his chair, Doctor Stephen Follansbee blotted the check, then, taking a bunch of keys from his pocket, he unlocked the top drawer of the desk and slipped the check into a small leather-bound book which lay inside.

"Just to make sure that I receive my just dues," he went on, "I'll turn this check in on Saturday instead of Monday. You're mad enough on one point, James Stone, but you're a shrewd man outside of that, and it might occur to you to stop payment on that check." His short, cackling laugh rang put anew.

Half an hour later he left his house. He did not seem to be in as much of a hurry as he had said, as he made his way leisurely, and on foot, to his destination.

He made a striking figure as he proceeded. His face alone would have attracted attention anywhere, but his dress was eccentric in its shabbiness. His arms were folded behind his back in a very unusual, but thoroughly characteristic way, and his little, lashless eyes were bent on the ground. Many passers-by stopped to stare at him as he passed, and not a few recognized him.

"He's the great Doctor Follansbee, the head of St. Swithin's Hospital!" they told one another. "You'd never think it to look at him, would you? He looks more like a mummy than anything else."

Careless of these comments and of the mild sensation his appearance always created, Follansbee soon reached the hospital, passed through the imposing entrance, and went on down the broad corridor to his private room. As soon as he had seated himself at his desk and glanced hastily through the few reports and other documents which lay there, he pressed one of several buzzer buttons on a small switchboard attached to his desk.

In response to the summons, the resident physician in charge quickly entered. Follansbee spent half an hour listening to the reports of the various cases and to matters of hospital routine. That done, he issued a few instructions in his sharp voice, and the physician left the room.

Other heads of departments followed, and for two hours Follansbee was constantly engaged. At the end of that time, though, he rose to his feet and passed through into an adjoining room which was fitted up as a private laboratory and workshop.

Crossing to one side of the room along which rows of shelves had been placed, he opened a small, glass-doored cupboard, and, leaning forward, took a small case of test tubes from one of the shelves, which contained serum of various types. Going back to his desk, the doctor seated himself and began to work. Evidently he was thinking something out with the aid of pencil and paper. He had a pad in front of him, and on it he scrawled a few lines of straggling writing. Then, after a prolonged pause, he jotted down a few more words.

"Yes," he said to himself presently, "I think that will be the best way. There's no reason why Crawford could not have been exposed to disease before his arrival. He has just landed in New York, and if I succeed in getting at him within the next day or so, there will be no reason for any one to suspect."

He leaned back in his chair.

"I'm sorry, though, that that mad fool attacked him," he went on musingly, "for, despite what Stone says, I feel sure that Crawford must be on his guard now."

That was the point in the case which baffled Follansbee for the moment. He could not understand why Crawford, after no less than three attempts had been made on his life, should still be willing to occupy a room which connected directly with that of his would-be murderer. At last, with a shrug of his shoulders, he dismissed the subject.

"After all, it doesn't matter very much," he mumbled to himself. "The attempts which Stone has made are only known to four or five persons at most. They are the two most concerned, young Floyd, and the stranger who, according to Stone's admission, separated him and Crawford on the boat. His knowledge and that of Floyd would be dangerous if Crawford were to be put out of the way in any ordinary fashion, but neither would be suspicious if he succumbed to a tropical disease. It would never occur to them to question his death under such circumstances, and even if it did, they wouldn't give Stone credit for so much ingenuity. As for me, I'm above suspicion, except in the eyes of a very few persons—notably Nick Carter's. I shouldn't like him to get wind of this, but there's little or no likelihood of his doing so."

James Stone had not known of the detective's identity, because the latter's name had not appeared on the passenger list of the *Cortez*, and, strictly speaking, it had been a breach of confidence on the part of the chief steward when the latter had revealed Carter's name to Crawford. Had Follansbee known more of the mysterious stranger whose intervention had been so unfortunate from Stone's standpoint, even his cold, hard calm would have been broken up, and he would have cut off his right hand rather than have anything to do with the affair. So far as his knowledge went, however, it seemed sufficiently safe to venture on what he had in view.

"Anyhow, I run no risk," he concluded. "Both Stone and Crawford seem to have no friends in the city, and if there should be a coroner's inquest the death would be put down as resulting from natural causes."

He ran his fingers over the test tubes with a touch that was almost caressing, and on his sallow, leathery face there rested a malevolent smile.

"My first step in the career of crime," he resumed, "was not very successful, I'll have to admit. It involved considerable risk, and I was infernally lucky to have crawled out of it as well as I did. I was a fool then, though, and I won't take any such risks in future. I'll be the 'man behind' this time. Stone will execute the work, and when it's duly accomplished, the reward will be mine, and I think I can worry along for some time on that amount."

Floyd, in his misguided effort to be thorough, had sent a number of details which might well have been omitted. They had enabled Follansbee to make a great show of knowledge, and by his evasions in respect to the source of it had greatly contributed to Stone's bewilderment. They had also made it possible for the un-scrupulous head of St. Swithin's to fill in the check for the amount that was only fifty thousand dollars short of the entire sum which Stone was supposed to have realized from the sale of the Condor Mine. He would have liked to claim even more, but he did not dare, for fear of overdrawing the miner's account and thereby creating a difficulty when the time came for the bank to honor the check. Therefore he had shrewdly fixed his "fee" at that sum, in order to allow for any reasonable withdrawals on Stone's part.

In that and other ways Floyd's letter had been of the greatest assistance, and had served a purpose the nature of which its writer had never dreamed. It would have seemed incredible to the young physician, whose profession was sacred to him, and in whose eyes Stephen Follansbee was everything that was desirable— except in external appearances.

Well he might. Few would have been willing to believe for a moment that the famous specialist could be guilty of such juggling with checks, and much less that he would consent to engage in a criminal conspiracy, the end of which was scien-tific murder, with any man—least of all one he knew to be mentally diseased. Yet, such was the fact.

Now and then a physician—sometimes a really great one—goes wrong and plays false to the tremendous responsibility which he has assumed. Stephen Fol-lansbee was one of the most conspicuous examples of this. He had started out with the highest motives, and worked his way up by hard work and sheer weight of ability. He had always been supremely selfish, however, and had possessed little or no heart. He had won fame in spite of his repellent appearance and his cold, unsympathetic nature. But that fame, and the reward which followed it, had not been enough for him. There was an evil streak in him, and it had become more pronounced as the years passed.

He had begun by using his position to cover up indefensible experiments on patients, especially those who were poor and obscure. Emboldened by his free-dom from penalty, he had gone on and indulged in more daring and ruthless work. Most of it had been in the name of medical knowledge, to be sure, and had had the sanction of not a few fellow practitioners, but it was none the less criminal.

At length, a year or so before, he had dared to try a particularly heartless experiment on a famous author, but while it was still in one of its early stages, Nick Carter had learned of it—it doesn't matter how—and had effectually interfered. Incidentally, the detective had prevented Follansbee from collecting fifty thousand dollars for his services, as he called them.

It had not been an indictable offense, and so Follansbee went unpunished. Carter had been obliged to content himself with a scathing denunciation, and a warning to keep straight in the future. To the best of the detective's knowledge, Follansbee had done so. This chance, however, had been too much for the distinguished scoundrel.

CHAPTER XII.

THE DEADLY TUBE.

While unconsciously playing into Follansbee's hands, Floyd had opened the way for a diabolical crime.

The head of St. Swithin's had adroitly pulled the wool over James Stone's eyes, and kept the half-crazed miner from knowing just what to expect; but nevertheless the specialist's mind had been made up from the beginning. He had planned it all out after receiving the letter.

As for his recognition of the miner, which had so startled his visitor, it had been a very simple matter, and quite within the capacity of one much less shrewd than Stephen Follansbee. Floyd had announced that Stone and Crawford had taken passage on the *Cortez*. Follansbee had taken pains to learn when the vessel had docked, and when, later, the big, bronzed man had presented himself, the caller's name had, to the doctor, been as good as written over his face.

That Stone was undoubtedly a victim of some mental derangement did not matter to Follansbee in the least. Almost any other physician would have been affected by the man's plight, and would have thought of nothing but the best way to cure him. Not so Follansbee, however. His apology for a heart had been hard in the beginning, and it had grown steadily harder as a result of his ostensibly scientific, but really devilish, experiments on unfortunate sufferers.

Had there been a spark of honor in him, he would have done all in his power to keep the irresponsible Stone from crime, and, if possible, to banish his ailment; but instead he determined to use the demented man for his own ends to help him to murder, and finally to strip him of his fortune.

His conscience had not given him a single twinge, for the very good reason that he had none. In fact, the prospective divisions of wealth seemed to him eminently right and proper. He might be taking away Stone's fortune, but he would be giving him Crawford's in place of it. In other words, he reasoned that Stone would be getting the job done for practically nothing, and the four hundred and fifty thousand, while generous pay, was not a cent too much according to Follansbee's view of it. He knew as well as any one could have known that, though he might try to shift the responsibility as much as he pleased, it lay with him, after all, and he wanted pay for it.

Moreover, he coveted wealth, more wealth than he had been able to amass through the many handsome fees that were pouring in all the time from the rich and great who were numbered among his patients. He wished to build a hospital of his own, of which he should be even more the master than was possible at St. Swithin's. He longed for expensive laboratories built and equipped along new lines, not for the good of humanity, but to further his own peculiar ambitions. Stone's money, with what he already possessed, would go far toward realizing these ambitions, and he was willing to take almost any risk to further his conscienceless aims.

The hours passed away swiftly, and at about seven o'clock in the evening Follansbee, returning from a round of the wards, entered his private office and went to the telephone. He rang up the Hotel Windermere and asked for Stone. The clerk informed him that Mr. Stone was not in the hotel at that time, but might return at any moment. "If you care to leave a message, it will be delivered to him as soon as he arrives," the man went on.

"Very well," Follansbee returned, after a pause. "Tell him that the gentleman whom he visited on Amsterdam Avenue this morning will be at the hotel about half past seven, and will wait for him in the lobby."

The clerk took down the message and repeated it, after which Follansbee replaced the receiver and prepared to leave the hospital. By means of an intercommunicating phone, he called up St. Swithin's garage and had his car, which he kept there, brought round to the entrance. As he crossed the pavement to enter it, he lifted one long, lean hand and pressed a smooth, round object in his breast pocket.

Little did the passers-by dream that, concealed in the clothing of that sinister, shabbily dressed, but nevertheless distinguished figure, was a tube containing deadly bacilli in a quantity sufficient to spread death for miles around—even, if unchecked, to sweep throughout the entire country.

Thus, like the shadow of death itself, the vulturelike form of Stephen Follansbee slipped into the big limousine, and was winged away to the Hotel Windermere.

CHAPTER XIII.

CHICK SIGHTS THE "BUZZARD."

"Who is it, please?"

Chick Carter, with his ear to the receiver, waited for the reply.

"This is Winthrop Crawford. I wish to speak to Mr. Nick Carter, if I may."

It was about two o'clock in the afternoon of the same day that had witnessed the meeting of Stone and Doctor Follansbee.

Unfortunately, Nick had just left the house, but his assistant had heard about Crawford.

"The chief isn't in just now, Mr. Crawford," he said, "but I don't think he'll be gone very long. Is there anything I can do for you? I'm his assistant."

"Are you the man who was with him on board the *Cortez*?"

"Yes."

"Perhaps you'll do as well, then. Are you busy just now?"

"No."

"Could you come down to the Hotel Windermere? I don't suppose it's very much, but I'd like to talk with one of you. I could come to your house, though, if you prefer."

There was no reason why Chick should not accept the invitation.

"No," he said. "I'll come down. I'm afraid I can't reach the hotel before three, though."

"Oh, that's all right; there's no particular hurry."

The detective replaced the receiver, saw to a few matters which demanded his attention, and then, after some twenty-five or thirty minutes, scribbled a brief message to his chief, and left it on the latter's desk—the usual information, telling where he had gone, and why.

Chick had never accustomed himself to riding in motor cars when it was unnecessary; therefore, he set out briskly for the nearest subway station.

"The chief seems very interested in Crawford," he thought, as he walked along. "We might as well get in touch with him as soon as we can."

He reached the Windermere a little after three, and found Crawford waiting for him in the lobby.

The bearded man seemed to be troubled about something, but his face brightened when Chick appeared. He led the way to one of the rooms which opened off the lobby. It proved to be deserted.

"It's nothing very important," Crawford explained, when they had seated themselves in a quiet, remote corner, "but I'm just a little troubled about my partner, Stone. He left the hotel immediately after breakfast this morning, and wouldn't tell me where he was going. He said he would be back in time for lunch, but he hasn't turned up yet." He glanced at Chick for a moment. "Of course. I'm not going to worry much about that," he went on, "but in case he doesn't appear by dinner time, I just wanted to know what to do. This New York of yours is a very bewildering place to a man who hasn't been in it for twenty-five or thirty years, and I would be at a loss to know how to proceed."

"Oh, that's easy enough," Chick said quietly. "If he doesn't show up by night, and you don't get a message, the best thing to do would be to ring up police headquarters and give a description of him. If anything had happened, they would be in a position to let you know sooner than any one else. They have the whole thing at their finger's ends down there, and handle ordinary cases with routine dispatch. You mustn't have any anxiety about Mr. Stone, though. He's surely able to take care of himself. He may have fallen in with some old friends, or made a new one."

"It does sound foolish, and I suppose you're right," Crawford admitted. "This place has got me scared, though. I have been used to solitude for a good many years, and the only crowds I've known have been those about the bars in mining camps. There must be a frightful number of accidents here every day."

He turned slightly in his chair and looked out through a near-by window into the traffic-filled street.

"You're free to laugh at me," he went on, "but I'm almost afraid to venture out alone. It looks to me as if a man has to take his life in his hands every time he crosses the street in this pandemonium." He paused again and smiled appealingly. "If you've got an hour or so to spare, would it be too much to ask you to pilot me around a bit?" he inquired. "I'd appreciate it, I assure you."

The deep, friendly voice had a certain charm in it which the detective found it impossible to resist.

"Of course I'll come gladly," he said.

He and Crawford left the hotel and strolled along the crowded pavements. The grizzled miner seemed to find a keen delight in halting to examine almost every window they passed.

"Spending years in the open makes a man fairly hungry for this sort of thing. I've longed to be back home again just to look into these very shop windows."

His enthusiasm was infectious, and he and Chick walked along, laughing and chatting together. They dropped in at the public library, and Crawford could hardly tear himself away.

When they reached the street again and started back toward Broadway, Chick happened to glance at a jeweler's clock.

"Half past five!" he ejaculated. "By George! I had no idea it was as late as that."

"Late be hanged!" Crawford answered, with a laugh. "The game is young yet. Let's have a look in at one of those continuous performances I've heard so much about—that is, unless you have to get back."

The detective had nothing pressing in view, and he was thoroughly enjoying Crawford's comments on what they saw. He, therefore, expressed his willingness to do whatever his companion wished, and conducted the latter to a combination moving-picture and vaudeville house, where they spent a little over an hour.

It was after seven when they returned to the hotel.

"I'll just go and see if Stone has come back," Crawford said anxiously. "I won't be long."

Chick nodded assent and seated himself in one corner of the lobby, while the miner made for the elevator.

Nick Carter's assistant had bought an evening paper and stuffed it into his pocket. He now took it out and began glancing over it.

Presently, as he lowered the paper to turn the page, his eyes chanced to look into a mirror set into the wall beside him. The mirror was so placed that it reflected the wide entrance of the hotel, and just at that moment Chick saw a lean, curious figure approach from the street. He gave a slight start, and stared for a moment at the familiar reflection, then instinctively raised the paper again so that it hid his face.

He never forgot features, and that one brief glance had been enough for him. As a matter of fact, however, there was little chance of any one forgetting Doctor Stephen Follansbee after even the most casual meeting.

"The 'Buzzard'!" he muttered to himself, using the name he had applied to the famous specialist. "I wonder what the dickens he's doing here."

CHAPTER XIV.

NICK'S ASSISTANT DECAMPS.

Chick knew all about Doctor Follansbee's tendencies, and had assisted his chief in an attempt to scrape up sufficient evidence against the man to warrant some definite action.

They had failed to build up a case that would amount to anything if brought to trial. To be sure, they could have brought charges against the head of St. Swithin's, and placed him before the medical association, but there was more than one reason for refraining from that. For one thing, Carter hesitated to stir up a scandal which would be bound to follow the publication of such charges. Owing to Follansbee's great prominence, and the very responsible character of his position as head of a big hospital, the accusation would tend to discredit the whole profession more or less, and to shake the public's faith in such institutions.

Finally, the detective had always been a firm believer in the right of a man to have a second chance, especially when he had much to lose. Follansbee had had his warning, and nothing had happened since to give the detective and his assistants any particular reason for believing that he had failed to profit by it. They were by no means sure that he had, however, and had continued to look out for further trouble in that direction; consequently, Chick was more than commonly interested in this chance glimpse of Follansbee.

As for his action in hiding himself behind the newspaper, that was merely a mechanical sort of routine precaution. There was always a certain possibility that Follansbee might be up to something questionable, and if he were in this instance the detective did not wish to be recognized. That would scare the game away, and his hunter's instinct shrank from the possibility of such a catastrophe.

Half a minute later he had cause to congratulate himself on his presence of mind.

He was not more than twenty feet from the clerk's desk, which Follansbee had approached.

"Is Mr. James Stone in?"

The question was put in the doctor's thin, piping voice, which hardly carried to Chick, and wrenched a little gasp of amazement from him.

"Stone!" he thought. "That can't be anybody but Crawford's partner. The Buzzard is asking for Stone. What does it mean?"

He strained his ears to catch the reply, but the clerk's voice was low and indistinct. A moment later, however, Follansbee remarked audibly: "All right, I'll wait for him here in this first sitting room for a few minutes."

Manipulating his paper cautiously, so that Follansbee could not see his entire face, even in the glass, Chick glanced at the latter with one eye. He was just in time to see the doctor move off and pass into one of the rooms which opened off from the lobby, the one nearest to the clerk's desk.

Chick felt instinctively that the discovery he had made was of considerable importance. He had come to look upon Follansbee with suspicion, and he was aware of Stone's attempts upon Crawford's life. To be sure, he also knew that Stone had been advised to consult a specialist in New York. It might well be, of course, that the specialist in question was Stephen Follansbee, and that the miner had gone to him in good faith. The connection between them, however, whatever it was, seemed to deserve a little more attention. At any rate, he felt that he ought to inform his chief at once of the fact that Follansbee had been inquiring for James Stone.

"I'll have to clear out of this," he thought, "and I mustn't let the Buzzard see me, either. If Crawford should come down and speak to me, Follansbee might be put on his guard—supposing there's anything fishy about his call on Stone. It's up to me to make tracks before Crawford comes back."

He rose to his feet, and as he did so the elevator bell gave a subdued buzz. The man in charge closed the gate, and the elevator shot upward. Chick felt morally certain that it was Crawford who had rung the bell, and was waiting to descend. Another might have laughed at him for the thought, when the big hotel was well filled with guests, but Chick put enough faith in it to cause his heart to give a startled bound. Without a look toward the elevator, he strode along the lobby in the direction of the door, and hurried out. He had barely disappeared when the car sank to the level of the ground floor, and Winthrop Crawford emerged.

The miner looked expectantly toward the corner where he had left Nick Carter's assistant, and stopped short when he found it vacant. His bewildered gaze traveled over the whole room, and then he approached a bell boy who was standing in a near-by doorway.

"Do you happen to know what's become of the young man I left in that corner less than five minutes ago?" he asked, pointing to the chair Chick had occupied.

"He's just gone out, sir," was the reply. "He hurried past me just before you came down, and shot out of the door as if he had been sent for."

"Did any one speak to him?"

"No, sir, not that I know. Maybe he just thought of something he had to do."

"That's queer!" Crawford muttered. "I don't understand it."

Then he suddenly made up his mind. "See if you can catch him," he said to the boy. "Hurry! There's a dollar in it if you do."

The bell boy broke into a run, and Crawford hastily followed. When he reached the street he saw the uniformed boy in full flight after a slender, well-dressed man who was walking swiftly down the street to the left. It looked like Chick, but in order to make no mistake, Crawford halted where he was and looked to the right, then crossed the street. He saw no one else whose appearance tempted him to follow; consequently, he strode in the wake of the boy. The latter soon caught up with his man and spoke to him. Crawford saw the pedestrian halt and turn about.

"Confound it!" the miner ejaculated under his breath, when he caught sight of the man's face. "That isn't my man. That fool boy has gone off on a wild-goose chase!"

He remained where he was and waited for the return of the bell boy, who came back sheepishly.

"It was the wrong man, sir," the boy explained.

"So I saw," was the answer. "Well, here's something for your trouble, anyway. I can't imagine how my friend got away so quickly."

"Thank you, sir!" said the boy, as he possessed himself of a coin. "Maybe he caught a car."

"That's probably what he did," agreed Crawford.

The boy left him and walked swiftly back to the hotel, but the miner followed much more slowly. He had been very favorably impressed by Chick and could not account for his sudden disappearance.

"Did I bore him as much as that?" he wondered. "He might at least have left some excuse, I should think, even if I had taken up too much of his time. If he had stayed he could have advised me about Jimmy."

He had failed to find Stone in his room, and the place seemed to indicate that his partner had not been there since morning. Yet, despite his anxiety, he was very reluctant to do anything, since he knew that if Stone were all right, he would greatly resent anything which looked like meddling with his affairs. When Crawford returned to the lobby of the Windermere, however, he found that his brief absence had brought developments.

These developments were to have considerable bearing on his affairs, although he was not to know of that for the present. While he was out of the building, Stone had returned, and had met Doctor Follansbee.

When Crawford reappeared, the clerk beckoned to him.

"Mr. Stone has just come in, Mr. Crawford, and has gone to his room with a friend," he was informed.

CHAPTER XV.

A BAD COMBINATION.

A look of great relief passed over Crawford's face as he thanked the clerk.

"Friend, eh?" he said to himself. "I didn't think he had a single one in these parts, except myself, and I'm afraid he doesn't think I'm his friend now."

The elevator was not at hand; consequently, he walked upstairs to the second floor. Passing along the corridor, he halted in front of number twenty-two and knocked.

"Who is that?" came the thick voice of James Stone.

"It's only Win Crawford," he returned, turning the knob of the door. He found it locked, however, and his partner's voice called out impatiently:

"I'm busy just now, and don't want to be disturbed."

With a shrug of his shoulders, and a return of the old troubled look on his face, Crawford turned away and went on to his own room to dress for dinner.

"Don't want to be disturbed," the mine owner thought, half bitterly. "There's no mistake about it. All of his old affection for me is dead. Heaven only knows how it's come about, but I'm sure it isn't my fault!"

Presently he was standing in front of his dresser, glancing mechanically at his bearded face in the mirror, and shaking his head.

"I'd give all I possess to find out what is the matter," he said. "Jimmy and I have been like brothers for years, and the way he's treating me now is almost more than I can bear. I sometimes wish we'd never found the mine, and were back again footing it through the bush together. We didn't have any money, and we never knew where the next meal was coming from, but—we were friends then."

As he crossed to the wardrobe he imagined he heard his name spoken, and came to a halt close to the connecting door. It was evident that the barrier was a thin one.

A murmur of voices came to his ear; but it was much too indistinct for him to make out any words. He could distinguish Stone's gruff tones, and also the sound of another voice—a much sharper, higher-pitched one. But that was all.

With an effort, Crawford roused himself and turned away. "Come, come!" he said to himself. "That isn't fair. You've never been an eavesdropper, and you're not going to turn to that sort of thing at your time of life."

He went on with his dressing, and at length heard the scrape of a key in the lock of the next door. Crossing to his own, Crawford opened it quietly and looked out. Stone was striding down the wide corridor, and by his side walked a thin, short, dried-up-looking individual.

As the two figures turned at the end of the corridor to go on down the stairs, the electric light at the landing shone for a moment full on the face of Stone's companion. Crawford had a glimpse of a bony jaw, a hooked, cruel nose, and a pair of small unprepossessing eyes.

"By George! What an ugly-looking fellow Jimmy has picked up!" the miner exclaimed, as he quickly withdrew his head, in order not to be seen spying on his old partner. "I wonder who the runt is, and where Jimmy got hold of him. They seemed to have something interesting to talk about."

He little dreamed that the subject they had found interesting was himself, and that the object of their conversation had been the devising of ways and means for taking his life.

The future, however, was to reveal it all to him, and, although he did not suspect anything at that moment there were others who did.

The bell boy had been right.

Chick had indeed run for a passing car and boarded it after emerging from the Windermere, and that explained his sudden disappearance from the street.

He had been so full of his discovery, and so anxious to escape from the hotel before Doctor Follansbee could see him and connect him with Crawford, that he had run a certain risk in dodging through the traffic and flinging himself on a moving trolley.

When he reached home a few minutes later, he found dinner waiting for him, and his chief and some of the others at the table.

"Hello, Chick!" was the greeting his chief gave him. "So you're back at last, are you? I got your message. Have you been with Crawford all this time?"

The young detective seated himself hastily, gave an account of the afternoon's program and then wound up with the startling information that he had heard Doctor Follansbee asking for Stone. At the mention of the specialist's name, Carter's lithe body stiffened, and he darted a quick glance at Chick.

"Follansbee and Stone!" he repeated. "That combination looks bad. I don't like it."

CHAPTER XVI.

A BIRD OF ILL OMEN.

"Neither did I," his assistant answered. "Don't forget, though, that that young doctor down in South America insisted that Stone should consult a specialist upon reaching New York. It looks as if Follansbee were the man."

"That seems probable," Nick agreed, "but it doesn't help matters very much. For all I know, Floyd may be a scamp himself, and even if he isn't, and has communicated with Follansbee in good faith, the latter may try some trick. Both Crawford and Stone are the sort of men who would be looked upon as easy marks. They've been out of the country for many years, and they now possess a million dollars between them. What's more, they're almost friendless here in New York. That fact would appeal to Follansbee. He made the mistake of aiming too high the last time—of trying to victimize a man who was too well known. If he hasn't turned over a new leaf—and I fear he hasn't—we may be pretty sure that he'll tackle a different proposition the next time."

"Well, I didn't feel easy about it," Chick admitted. "That's why I hurried out without waiting for Crawford to return."

A brief silence fell between them, although some of the others at the table renewed in lower tones the conversation which Chick's entrance had interrupted. The chief was eating mechanically and hurriedly, and the absent-minded expression on his face told Chick that something was in prospect.

Presently the detective refused his dessert, and rose to his feet. "What's the number of Crawford's room at the Windermere?" he asked.

"Twenty-one," Chick answered.

Carter went out into the hall, where the nearest of the several telephone connections in the house was located. The listening Chick heard him shuffling over the pages of the directory, and then caught the click as the receiver was removed from its hook. The chief gave a number, and after a little delay asked: "Is this the Windermere?" In another moment he went on: "I wish to engage a room for a few days, and I'm particular about its location. Is number twenty-two vacant?"

A slight grin parted his assistant's lips. "It isn't?" he heard his chief ask. "Then how about twenty?" There was another pause, and then: "Good! I'll take it. Mortimer is the name—Thomas Mortimer. Got that? Thanks!"

In a moment Carter put his head in at the dining room door. "I'd like to see you in the study when you get through," he said to Chick. "Don't hurry, though.

There's time enough."

His assistant did justice to the meal, but wasted no time in conversation with the rest. Fifteen minutes later he went up to the study and found his chief seated at the desk.

"You think Crawford is in danger, then?" Chick asked, as he entered.

Carter's face was grave. "I fear he is," he said. "Something tells me that I may be called on to save our friend's life again before long—or try to. It's more than possible, of course, that my suspicions are groundless. It isn't likely that Stone knew Follansbee was a crook before he called on him. He may not know it now, and Follansbee may not be planning anything out of the way. The situation is full of sinister possibilities, however, and I feel compelled to get on the ground without much delay. It promises to be a complicated affair. If Follansbee is running straight, all well and good. On the other hand, he may be planning to victimize one or the other of the partners, or both."

Chick nodded. "He's quite capable of doing them both," he agreed.

"There's no doubt about that," Carter went on. "I hope I'm wrong, but I have come to look upon him as a bird of ill omen. Whenever his vulturelike face appears, I'm inclined to take it as a sign of impending trouble. If I misjudge him, I'm sorry, but I don't intend to be caught napping this time if I can help it."

"And you're really going to stay at the Windermere for the present, chief?"

"Yes, that's the least I can do. If Stone has joined forces with Follansbee, Crawford will have little chance against them. It would not be so bad if Crawford would only realize his danger, and would consent to take proper precautions. As you know, though, he has already experienced no less than three attacks on the part of his old partner, and yet he still sticks by him. I can't help admiring the man for his loyalty, but it's very quixotic, and I feel that I'll have to guard him from himself."

"Are you going to tell Crawford that you're coming to the hotel to live?"

Nick shook his head decidedly.

"By no means," he returned. "Crawford is much too simple-minded a man for that, and is more than likely to give me away. I shall disguise myself to-night before I go there, and you'll have to hold the fort here while I'm away. Of course, you can communicate with me whenever you have to."

Chick's face changed its expression.

"But you'll give me a chance to take a hand in this affair as soon as the time is ripe, won't you, chief?" he pleaded. "I didn't come out with flying colors from our previous bout with Follansbee, and I'd like to get another crack at him."

The chief was at the door of the study now, and he turned and nodded to his assistant, a slight smile playing about his lips.

"All right!" he answered. "You'll have a chance, I promise you, if the case shapes up as I anticipate."

CHAPTER XVII.

NICK CARTER MISCALCULATES.

At seven o'clock on the evening of the twenty-fourth the dining room of the Hotel Windermere presented a scene of animation. The big hotel was fairly well filled, and most of its guests, as well as many outsiders, seemed to be on hand.

At a table in one of the little alcoves sat a quietly dressed gentleman in evening clothes. A close-clipped, iron-gray mustache adorned his lips, and the hair on his temples was tinged with gray, which contrasted with the deep tan of his hands and neck. He was known in the hotel as Thomas Mortimer, a wealthy traveler and sportsman.

From where he sat, Nick—as we may as well call him—could see the table at which Crawford and Stone usually seated themselves. He had been in the hotel constantly, and had kept a sharp watch on Stone's movements, but the miner's actions had puzzled him not a little. Several times he had met Stone stalking along the corridor or in the lobby, his brows knitted, and his lips moving as if he were talking to himself.

Nick had been too clever to thrust his companionship on the man, and Stone did not even know that "Mortimer" had a room so near to his own. It was not part of the detective's policy to allow Stone, or the more subtle-minded Follansbee, to have a chance to penetrate his disguise.

So far, however, he had not been able to find out anything that was likely to help him in his self-imposed task of guarding the life of Winthrop Crawford. Follansbee had not reappeared at the Windermere, and although there was every possibility that Stone had been holding some sort of communication with the scoundrelly physician, the detective had not been able to discover the means by which he did so.

Crawford, on his part, had been busy. Several men had called on him at the hotel, evidently to urge the advantage of certain investments, and one or two had been closeted with the miner for several hours. It was obvious that he was trying to find a safe channel for some of his money, and probably at the same time seek an outlet for his own energies. He was not a man who would be likely to settle down and be content to do nothing.

James Stone, however, seemed to be of a different type, or else his insane suspicions of his former partner kept him in a state of mind which prevented him from seeking new business responsibilities.

Nick noted that Stone was the first to take his seat at the table. Crawford did not put in an appearance until a few minutes later, and by that time his partner had already finished the first course. The two men exchanged a few monosyllables as the meal went on, and as soon as he had finished, Stone rose with only the curtest of nods to his partner.

Nick had already signed the waiter's slip, but had been toying with a little fruit. He rose and followed Stone, but without any sign of hurrying. His man used the stairs, and the detective followed in the elevator, reaching the second floor ahead of his quarry.

Nick's room, number twenty, occupied an angle of the corridor, its door being almost opposite the elevator, while those leading to the rooms occupied by Stone and Crawford were just around the corner.

When the detective entered his room, he left his door slightly ajar, and a few moments later he heard Stone's footsteps, as the miner passed and went on round the angle. Nick gently closed his door and crossed his room to the window, without turning on the lights.

The window looked out into a big courtyard of the Windermere, and from it, by glancing sharply to his right, Nick could see the window of Crawford's bedroom, and also that of Stone's, both of which were not on a line with his, but at right angles.

Peering out through the darkness, he saw a light leap up suddenly in Stone's room, and presently the shadow of a man appeared on the shade.

The moving shadowgraph was significant. The detective inferred from Stone's actions that he must be putting on a light overcoat.

"He seems to be going out again," the detective commented mentally. "And in that case, I'd better go ahead again."

He stepped back from the window, hurriedly snapped on the electric lights, and secured his own hat and walking stick. That done, he left the room, locked the door behind him, and made for the stairs. No one followed, and he concluded that something had delayed Stone.

The detective slowed down and leisurely entered the lobby. He seated himself there after buying a paper at the news stand; but ten minutes passed without any sign of James Stone.

"What is keeping him?" he wondered. "Can it be that he sneaked out through one of the other entrances?"

The thought was a disagreeable one, and Nick decided to put it to the test at once, without further delay. He climbed the stairs once more, hurriedly entered his own room, and crossed to the window.

A glance to the right told him that his suspicion was well founded. There was no light in Stone's room now, and it was obvious that the tall miner had left.

CHAPTER XVIII.

ON THE FIRE ESCAPE.

An exclamation of annoyance broke from Nick Carter's lips.

"I didn't give him credit for so much cunning," he thought. "But hanged if I see why he should have felt it necessary to skulk away in that fashion. It can't be possible that he suspects me, and I don't know of any reason why Crawford should not know of his going out."

He concluded on the whole that it was probably an evidence of the instinctive slyness of the mentally affected, and nothing more. Further, he concluded that Stone had probably turned along the corridor in the other direction, used the servants' stairs, and left by one of the side exits. Of course, it was possible that his demented brain had urged him on to the use of the fire escape. The more he thought about it, the more he became convinced that the latter supposition was nearer the truth. It would be just like a man in Stone's condition to resort to such a ruse.

The miner's disappearance had been a great disappointment to the detective. When he had discovered from the shadows on the drawn shade that Stone was going out, his hopes had risen. He had counted on following the man and getting some line on his movements, but now that was out of the question.

He knew that it was useless to follow Stone after that delay, but as a result of a few seconds' deliberation, he decided not to let the chance slip altogether. Donning his lightweight overcoat, and buttoning it up to his chin in order to conceal the conspicuous expanse of white shirt front—which might draw undesired attention—he softly raised the sash of his window and stepped out on the wide sill. The fire escape did not lead down directly past his room, but one end of the iron platform came within two or three feet of the window on the right side.

It was the simplest matter in the world for Nick to grasp the rail and to hoist himself over.

The windows of the hotel were supplied with a novel patent catch which automatically fastened both the upper and lower sashes when the latter was pulled down. Nick, therefore, took pains to leave his window open after passing through it.

It was this peculiarity of the windows which had brought him out on the fire escape. He knew that if Stone had his wits about him, and had departed by that route, he must have left his window open or fixed it in some way to prevent his being locked out. It was to find if such precautions had been taken that he had made the effort.

When he approached Stone's window, the lower sash seemed to be closed, but a closer inspection revealed that a narrow wedge of wood had been inserted, leaving a half-inch crack at the bottom—just enough to permit a man's fingers to get a purchase on the sash and raise it.

It was only a trivial thing, but it gave Nick a clew to what was going to happen.

"He didn't want the window to be locked by accident," he mused, "and so he placed the wedge there. That means he's going to come back this way, and it seems to me also that he wishes his partner to think he has been in all the evening—probably that he has gone to bed. It looks as if things were coming to a head."

There was a cluster of small lights on a pole in the middle of the big courtyard, and the shades of many of the windows opening on it were up. It was light enough, therefore, for the detective to see with reasonable clearness—and to be seen, if any one happened to look in his direction.

He leaned over the rail and peered down. He was only at the level of the second floor, but the pavement of the courtyard was flush with the basement; therefore, two floors beneath him. He looked to see if the lowest ladder of the fire escape was in place but saw that it was not.

"Stone probably dropped from the last platform," he concluded. "It wouldn't have been anything for a man of his active habits. I wonder how he expects to get back, though. By George! There's a painter's ladder lying on the pavement on the other side of the court. Such things never ought to be left around. The sight of that ladder would tickle a thief to death. Stone probably saw it and made his plans accordingly.

"He expects to use it to reach the lower platform, but I'm curious to know what else is in his mind. According to Crawford he's sane enough in all respects but one—and he wasn't born yesterday. He must know that he can't leave the ladder set up against the landing when he comes back to his room. If he does, there will surely be an investigation in the morning, if not before. Does he merely think that there will be a little burglar scare which won't affect him, or is there something deeper in all this?

"Has he gone off half-cocked, or—— Great Ned! I wonder if that can be it. If he were going to bring some one back with him—some one who would be leaving by the same route later on who could put the ladder back where it was originally—that would effectually remove the difficulty. If Stone is as shrewd as I give him credit for being, I'll wager that's what's in the wind. And I can give a guess at his prospective visitor's identity."

He referred, of course, to Doctor Follansbee; and the possibility that the latter was expected later on that night was enough to stir his pulses. It suggested that the period of inactivity was about to come to an end, and that the test of his unsolicited guardianship of Winthrop Crawford was at hand.

Stone had gone, and it was unnecessary, as well as useless, to attempt to follow him. All that remained was to await his return as patiently as possible, and in the meantime to keep an eye—or at least, an ear—out for Crawford.

The latter proved an easy matter, for about an hour later he heard the door of Crawford's room open and close, and from his window saw the light flash up in his new friend's.

A glance at his watch told him that it was now almost ten o'clock. He knew that Crawford was a man who rose early, and there was every probability that the miner was about to turn in for the night.

Nick's own room had remained in darkness. He now drew a chair close to his window and took up his vigil, his arms resting on the sill. Fifteen or twenty minutes later the light vanished in Crawford's room. In order to make sure, the detective hurriedly rose, slipped to his own door, and opened it slightly. His friend did not appear in the corridor, which was sufficient proof that he was going to bed.

Nick reclosed his door and locked it. "You are settled for the night," he thought; "and now for Stone."

He was possessed of the infinite patience that means so much to a detective, and is so essential to the success of any one who takes up that profession. The rumble of traffic gradually died down, and light after light went out in the hotel. At last, in the distance the clock in the Metropolitan tower struck twelve. Yet the bunch light still glowed in the courtyard below, and many windows were rectangles of light, bright or subdued, as the case might be, for New York is very slow to go to bed.

The detective's lower sash was raised about six or eight inches, and that fact at length enabled him to hear a slight sound in the courtyard, even before his watchful eyes had warned him of the approach. He did not make the mistake of leaning out of the window. Indeed, it would not have been easy to do so, in view of the narrow space he had left.

In any case, it was unnecessary. The painter's ladder was well within his range of vision, and a few moments later he had the satisfaction of seeing two figures steal into view and grasp it. They had come from the open end of the courtyard, which was on Nick's side, and out of his sight.

They picked up the ladder and started to sidle across the court in the direction of the fire escape. There was more than a hint of sinister purpose in their furtive movements, and an instant later first one and then the other raised his head and scanned the tiers of windows above, as if to make sure that they were not observed.

As they did so, the lights of the cluster fell on their faces for a fleeting instant, and the muscles of Nick's jaws tightened. He had barely glanced at the taller figure. It was the shorter, slightly stooped one which interested him most, and he had seen all that was necessary.

The second man wore the repellent mask of Stephen Follansbee.

CHAPTER XIX.

A FIENDISH PLOT.

The two skulkers soon disappeared, having drawn too close to the nearer wall for Nick Carter to see them. He put his ear close to the opening, however, and listened.

He was enabled to hear the ladder placed against the fire escape, faint though the sound was, and to check off the men's movements as they climbed upward. When they approached the second floor, he quietly slipped out of his chair and retreated into the shadows in the middle of the room. He did not care to be seen at the window, even though his identity was so well cloaked.

Apparently no word was exchanged on the part of the two climbers. They were running a considerable risk, and they doubtless knew it. There was quite enough light for them to be seen if any one should look out of one of the many windows which opened on the court. Fortunately for them, however, they did not have far to go, and were not obliged to pass a single bedroom.

They made their way upward with a great deal of care, but Nick could plainly hear the faint scrape of their shoes on the metal steps.

It was obvious that they had already settled all the details.

"They have everything cut and dried," the detective told himself, his keen eyes glinting in the shadows, "and men of their type do not go to such deliberate pains for nothing."

After that the sounds told the detective that the first man, probably Stone himself, had reached the landing just to the right of his window, and almost immediately afterward he caught the faint noise made as the sash was raised.

There was a little more rustling and scraping, then silence. The detective concluded that it was safe enough to return to his point of vantage outside. Just as he did so, he saw the lower sash of Stone's window being pulled down.

"I hope they leave that wedge in place," he murmured.

The light flashed up, and the shade was drawn down—by Doctor Follansbee, as the shadow showed.

There was no way of telling, however, whether the wedge had been removed or not. Follansbee had doubtless been the last to pass through, and probably did not know of its existence; and then it might have been dislodged by the passage of one or the other of them.

It was time for the watcher to become the man of action, and the transformation entailed considerable risk, as the detective knew. He did not mean to remain in idleness where he was; but, on the contrary, had determined to repeat his maneuver of some time before. In other words, he meant to crawl out on the fire escape once more and take a position outside of the miner's window, in the hope that he could hear enough of the conversation between the two to enable him to get a clew to their intentions, if not with regard to Winthrop Crawford.

The sounds they had made with all their care had brought his danger home to him, and he realized that the necessity for climbing over the iron railing made it likely that he would cause even more noise. The attempt must be made, though, come what might, and Nick had already made preparations for it. He had anticipated the necessity, and had previously transferred a little instrument from one of his suit cases to his pocket.

It was a sort of disc made of hard rubber for the most part, and about an inch in thickness. Its use was obscure at first glance, but would have been sufficiently plain upon examination. It was a sort of ear trumpet designed for the deaf, but without the old-fashioned horn attachment.

He buttoned his coat once more about him, then proceeded to raise his window the required distance; but at the risk of missing something important, he took his time about it, with the result that the slight sound could not have been heard even a few feet away. When there was room enough for him to crawl through, he did so, and, leaning over, grasped the end of the platform. He stepped noiselessly across the gap, threw one leg over the railing and gently lowered himself to the grating. Along this he tiptoed, his thin-soled shoes making practically no sound as he advanced. In a few moments he was kneeling in front of Stone's window with the rubber disc held to his right ear, and his ear lowered to the crack at the bottom of the sash.

The wooden wedge was still in place, luckily for him, consequently the sash had remained slightly raised. As soon as the device was brought into use, it amplified the sounds it caught, and what had been an indistinct murmur of voices became an easily audible conversation.

"Be very careful of this," were the first definite words he heard. They were in Doctor Follansbee's voice. "I will leave it in the case here for you," the high, thin tones went on. "Don't press the plunger until you have inserted the needle underneath the skin. Is that clear?"

"Yes."

The detective hardly recognized Stone's voice, so hoarse and agitated did it sound.

"The drug and sponge will be easy for you to handle," Follansbee explained. "Wait until you get into the room and are six feet or so from the bed, then just sprinkle a few drops on the sponge from this vial."

"Won't he smell the stuff and wake up?"

"Certainly not, unless you make a noise. The drug has a penetrating odor, of course, for the time being, but his sleeping sense won't convey a message of warning soon enough to spoil your plans. If the odor reaches his nostrils before you're ready to act, and he's really asleep, it will probably only cause a momentary dream of some sort; an attempt of the subconscious self to explain the situation."

"All right, but—but won't they be able to tell that he's been drugged?"

Nick heard a thin, piping laugh. "You must think me a fool," Follansbee's voice returned. "The keenest scent would be incapable of detecting any odor in the room five minutes after that drug is used, and it leaves little or no after effects. Crawford will wake up to-morrow morning without the slightest suspicion that anything has happened to him, and he'll feel perfectly normal."

"And what about the—the other?"

"It will not begin to show itself until Monday or Tuesday," was the confident answer. "And even then the symptoms will be inconclusive. There aren't half a dozen physicians who would know what they meant in any of the early stages, and by the time any one could authoritatively diagnose the case, the patient would be beyond help. In fact, he'll be beyond it for all ordinary purposes from the time the serum is introduced into his system, and before the twenty-seventh he'll be dead."

CHAPTER XX.

QUICK WORK IS NECESSARY.

"Dead!"

The way in which Stone repeated the word gave a hint to the listener of the grim hatred that possessed that demented brain.

There was a moment's silence, then Follansbee's voice came again. "Above all, however," he said, "remember that you must not be in a hurry. Do everything deliberately and don't get rattled for a moment. There's nothing to fear if you keep your nerve. Finally, don't attempt to carry out your—operations shall we call it?—until half past two."

"Why should we wait? Why couldn't we do it now?" Stone urged.

"If you were a medical man you would know why," Follansbee answered in his squeaking voice. "Between two and three o'clock in the morning human life is at its lowest ebb. The flame of vitality burns more dimly then than at any time during the twenty-four hours. That's the answer, and its application to this case ought to be apparent enough."

Nick heard a movement, as though Doctor Follansbee had leaned forward in his chair to drive his point home.

"You have waited months for this, Stone," the peculiar voice went on, "and an hour more or less can't make any difference. Crawford will be in a sound sleep at half past two, if he's as normal as he seems to be, and the low vitality which is natural at that hour will make him an easy subject to handle; in other words, you will have the best chance of successfully drugging him."

The chair creaked again.

"You're going now?" asked the miner.

"Yes. It's much better that I should. My continued presence would tempt us to talk, and we might disturb the man in the next room. You don't want to do that, you know. You want to find him as helpless as possible when the time comes, so I'd advise you to keep as still as you can. Don't pace the room, or anything like that."

"But I'm nervous as a cat," objected Stone. "Who wouldn't be?"

"I suppose you are," Follansbee admitted, "but—here's something to quiet you. It will give you new courage, too. Just deposit this powder on the end of your tongue and wash it down with a little water."

There was a pause, and the detective suspected that the miner was staring questionably at Follansbee. Stone's next words confirmed it.

"You're sure about this?" the man asked slowly. "It won't hurt me or keep me from doing what I've sworn to do?"

"Certainly not," was the shrill response. "What do you take me for, Stone? I'm in your pay, am I not? I must earn that forty-five thousand, if I expect to enjoy it. Why should I try any tricks on you?"

"That's all right—why should you?" Stone said more quietly. "I'll take it if it will fix me up in the way you say. Here goes!"

The detective outside held his breath. "Great Scott!" he thought. "I wonder if Follansbee is putting up a job on him, too. He'd be quite capable of it, but it doesn't seem possible that he's trying any such tricks so early in the game. If he means to do anything of that sort, I should think he would wait until Stone had killed his partner, or had attempted to do so. To Follansbee's certain knowledge, that would give the latter a hold on Stone which Follansbee could use to advantage before going any further. I may be mistaken about that, of course. Follansbee does strange things, and may have something up his sleeve which I don't understand. There's a chance that Stone is in grave danger at this moment. I doubt it, though, and I'm afraid I can't help him if he is."

Nick's main concern was to protect Winthrop Crawford if possible. He pitied Stone much more than he blamed him, because he knew that the man was not responsible for his actions, but Crawford's life was more important than Stone's, and a premature interference might spoil the case that was developing against Doctor Follansbee.

"That will steady you," he heard the specialist inform Stone. "I'm off now, and remember that I shall be waiting for you in front of the bank around the corner. I'll have a car there in readiness at two-thirty. I trust you told the hotel people that you would probably be away to-night?"

"Yes, I arranged that. I didn't see why it was necessary, but— —"

Had the detective been able to look into the room, he would have found that Follansbee was facing his man, but that Stone was not quick enough to notice the cold flicker that came into the hard eyes. The detective would have perceived it, though, had he been in a position to do so, and would have jumped to the conclusion that the rascally physician had a reason of his own for wanting Stone to join him as soon as the dastardly crime had been committed.

"My reason is very obvious," Follansbee declared in his thin, cackling voice. "I want you to establish an alibi in case something unexpected should happen."

He thrust his face forward.

"You don't want to be electrocuted, do you?" he demanded. "That would be a poor sort of revenge on your partner."

Nick heard the ex-miner draw a deep breath.

"Electrocuted!" came the deep, husky voice. "I don't think I'd care for that. They — they would send me to the chair, though, wouldn't they, if they found out?"

Follansbee knew better than that. He was aware that Stone would escape any such fate owing to his mental condition, but it did not suit his purposes to say so. "As sure as you're alive!" he answered callously.

As he spoke, he turned to the window and started for it.

It was not the sound of his approaching footsteps that warned the listener, however. Nick had already stiffened and drawn back as soon as his ears caught the difference in Follansbee's tones, caused by the fact that the latter had faced about toward the window while in the act of making his last remark.

The thin, stunted shadow of the head physician of St. Swithin's was already on the shade, and quick work was necessary on Nick's part.

CHAPTER XXI.

IN NEED OF EVIDENCE.

Nick Carter moved with the quickness of a cat. In a twinkling he had jerked the ear piece away and slipped it into his pocket. While doing so, he had straightened up noiselessly and started along the platform of the fire escape in the direction of his own window.

It was a close shave. Follansbee had started to raise the shade before Nick even reached the railing over which he had to climb, and while he was crawling over the barrier the sash of Stone's window was being lifted.

Fortunately for him, however, Follansbee tried to make as little noise as possible, consequently his movements were slower than they otherwise would have been. For all that, though, the detective was not out of sight by the time Follansbee stuck his head and shoulders through the opening.

It was a tense moment, and Nick's heart skipped a beat or two. Should Follansbee happen to glance that way the first thing and catch a glimpse of his feet disappearing through the window the consequences would be disastrous.

Despite the temptation to do so, he did not forget his caution for a moment, or allow his extreme haste to betray him into a clumsy move. He slipped from view almost noiselessly, and tiptoed away from his window into the shadows of his room.

All the time he was listening intently for some evidence that Follansbee had seen him, but none came. Seemingly the physician continued to climb through Stone's window, and, having done so, proceeded on his stealthy way down the fire escape.

The detective heard a slight sound, followed by the grating of the sash. Evidently the ex-miner had again closed the window.

As soon as Nick dared, he ventured back and stealthily peered over his own sill. Follansbee was then descending the painter's ladder. And when the bottom was reached, he lifted the ladder carefully away from the lower platform of the fire escape and carried it, with considerable difficulty, back to the place from which it had been taken.

Subsequently his figure vanished, going in the direction of the open end of the court.

"The end of the first act," thought Nick, "and the play promises to be a hair-raiser."

With his brows drawn together and his arms folded across his breast, he paced softly up and down his room, turning his discoveries over and over in his mind. He had heard enough to realize that Crawford was in deadly peril. With his usual cunning, Stephen Follansbee had again taken what promised to be a perfectly, safe course. To the specialist's crooked brain, there could be no possible chance of fixing the contemplated crime on him, if it was Stone, the tool, who was playing the principal part.

To be sure, Nick had overheard a conversation which left him in no doubt as to where the real responsibility lay. He had heard Follansbee say that as a result of the proposed measures, Crawford would be dead before the twenty-seventh. To the uninitiated, that would have seemed conclusive, and more than enough to convict the physician. Nick Carter knew better, however; at any rate, he knew enough to be sure that Follansbee would make a great fight if the case ever came to trial, and might easily wriggle out of it.

In the first place, he was a distinguished man, a leading light in his profession, and the ruling spirit of a great hospital. Nick was the only witness, and it would be very hard, if not impossible, for the detective, with all his reputation, to convince a jury on the strength of such evidence alone that Doctor Stephen Follansbee would stoop to become the accessory to a murder.

Follansbee would have the advantage of dealing with a demented man, and could insist that everything which seemed suspicious about his actions — the use of the fire escape and all — had been due to that fact. In other words, he might build up a plausible excuse on the theory that he had been humoring Stone in order to study his case, and to see how far the miner's insanity would carry him.

"It must be the germ of some deadly disease, characteristic of the tropics," Nick told himself, "and he has left the hypodermic syringe there for Stone to use. That's as plain as the nose on my face. But without more evidence than I now have, I can't be sure of securing a conviction. Follansbee is as shrewd as they make them. I wouldn't be a bit surprised to have him claim that the contents of the syringe were harmless, and that he was merely 'stringing' Stone for some medical reason. What he said about Crawford's death could always be attributed to the same motive, and his reputation is so great that it would probably hypnotize a jury into accepting his word for it. He's a cunning rascal, and no mistake. How am I going to manage this affair? I've got to do something before two-thirty, but what?"

It was seldom that Nick Carter felt at a loss, yet he realized that his position was a peculiarly difficult one. He might have forced his way into James Stone's room, of course, but he felt that the mine owner would have sufficient cunning to destroy at once the only tangible evidence of guilt as soon as he heard the first alarm. And even if he did foil Stone's attempt that night, the detective feared that it would only be putting off the evil day. He could have Stone locked up, to be sure, and an inquiry into his sanity begun. He might also be able to secure Follansbee's arrest.

That would seem to clear the way and remove Crawford's danger; but the detective saw further than that. He felt certain that Follansbee must have demanded a large fee of Stone, either for treatment or frankly for the services of getting rid of the man's partner. Furthermore, he was assured that Follansbee had contrived it so that the fee would be paid whatever happened.

In that case the arrest or death would by no means end the matter. Follansbee's professional standing would undoubtedly result in an arrangement whereby the specialist would go free under heavy bonds pending his trial, and the moment he was at liberty to do so, he would almost certainly begin work on a new attempt to get rid of Winthrop Crawford and to earn his money.

That fact had to be taken into consideration in connection with Follansbee, for the latter would not be treated as an ordinary criminal; therefore, it became increasingly evident that Nick would have to meet cunning with cunning if he hoped to handle the affair successfully.

At last, the hint of a plan came to him. He halted by his window and looked out again. The light was still shining in Stone's room. "I must go in there without the fellow's knowledge," he thought. "A minute, possibly half a minute, would do, with good luck. I wonder how I can manage it, though?"

CHAPTER XXII.

HELP FROM THE HOUSE DETECTIVE.

Nick looked at his watch. It was ten minutes of one.

More than an hour and a half remained before half past two. There seemed to be plenty of time, therefore; but he could not be sure that Stone would take Follansbee's advice and wait until that hour before attacking his partner. The man's insane impatience might get the upper hand and lead him to act before the time set. But the plan which had come to Nick could be put into execution at once, and thus a nerve-racking delay could be avoided.

The detective might have acted wholly on his own responsibility, but many difficulties would have been involved in that case, and he decided against it. He turned on the lights in his room and looked up at the wall in the neighborhood of the door. As he had anticipated, his eyes fell upon an electric bell, which had doubtless been placed there in order to arouse guests who might have left instructions for an early call. If there was one in his room, there was doubtless one in each of the others—including James Stone's. Having made up his mind as to that, the detective switched off the light again, softly unlocked and opened his door, and slipped out into the corridor.

The Hotel Windermere was a modern one, with all the latest safeguards, including floor clerks; in other words, there was a clerk on each floor night and day. These clerks had desks in the main corridors, with mirrors about them so arranged that they could see what went on in all of the side passages. Calls from their floor were handled by them, and it was their business to see that everything was orderly and respectable, to scrutinize visitors, to note the comings and going of guests, and to keep a watch for delinquencies on the part of employees.

Nick approached the clerk on his floor, a young woman of thirty-three or four.

"Will you kindly tell me where I can find the house detective at this hour?" he asked.

The clerk looked him over in some surprise. "Has anything happened?" she asked quickly. "Have you lost anything?"

Nick smiled slightly. "Oh, no," he answered. "It's nothing of that sort. I simply have business with your detective." As he spoke, he took out a two-dollar bill and laid it on the young woman's desk. "And I must ask that you look upon my interest in him as strictly confidential," he added.

The clerk frowned slightly as she saw the money, then gave the detective a searching look. "I can't accept that, Mr. Mortimer," she said, giving him the name he was using at the hotel. "We clerks are not allowed to accept tips. It wouldn't do, you know. Thank you just as much, though. You may be sure I won't say anything about it. You'll find Mr. Stickney, the detective, in room twelve hundred and twelve."

"Thanks," Nick replied. "And accept my apologies, please. I didn't think for a moment of the policy here. I don't want to go up to the detective's room, though, for that would arouse the curiosity of the elevator boy. Will you kindly telephone and ask him to meet me here as soon as he can?"

"Certainly," was the reply.

Ten minutes later, the house detective, having dressed hastily, put in an appearance. Nick greeted him and drew him aside. He knew Stickney, but had not seen fit to reveal that fact to the floor clerk.

"Look here, Stickney," he said, as soon as they were out of earshot, "I suppose you wonder what you're up against. I'm registered here under the name of Thomas Mortimer, but you know me better as Nick Carter."

Stickney gave a low whistle. "For the love of Mike!" he ejaculated under his breath. "Let me have a good look at you. Yes, I guess you're Nick all right, although I wouldn't have dreamed of it if I'd passed you a dozen times. What's the matter? Is there anything queer going on here?"

Nick nodded. "Very queer," he answered. "This isn't the proper time to go into particulars, but I'll tell you this much. The man in number twenty-two has a room or two to rent in his upper story, and if you're not careful he's going to commit a terrible crime this very night. There are reasons for keeping dark, and for not taking him into custody just yet. Will you help me, though, to save him from himself, and to shield his intended victim?"

"Sure thing!" was the prompt answer. "I'll do anything I can. I'd like to know a little more about it, and I'd insist if you were any one else. I can trust you, though, and I'll keep mum until you give me the word. What is it you want?"

"Something very simple."

Nick drew nearer to the house detective and spoke even lower. "Do you get the idea?" he asked, in conclusion.

Stickney nodded. "Of course," he answered. "I can fix that up without any trouble. Is that all you want me to do?"

"That's all," Nick replied. "Wait for ten minutes after I get back to my room, and then let it go. I'll be ready to take advantage of the opportunity. Keep out of sight yourself, and tip off our young friend at the desk, so that she'll know what to do when Stone complains. Tell her to keep the whole affair quiet. I'll let you know in due time how I've succeeded; and if I need any more help later on I'll surely call upon you."

"I get you," declared the house detective, and turned briskly away.

Nick Carter quietly returned to his own room, locked himself in, and went to his window. Stone's light was still burning, but Crawford's window was as dark as before. To all appearances, Stone was biding his time as Follansbee had advised.

The detective consulted his watch once more, made a few preparations, and then, stationing himself finally at his open, unlighted window, awaited the prearranged signal. At the end of ten minutes a startling din came to his ears from near at hand, and he prepared for action.

The time had come.

CHAPTER XXIII.

THE HYPODERMIC.

The detective's scheme was simplicity itself, and it promised success. He had merely instructed Stickney to have Stone's bell rung at the appointed time, and to keep it ringing continuously until the miner should leave his room in desperation to complain of the nuisance.

If it worked out as Nick hoped, Stone's absence would give him the opportunity he sought, and meanwhile the miner would be informed that the electrical apparatus must have been deranged in some way. It would be looked to and "remedied;" whereupon, the ringing would cease, and Stone would receive the apologies of the management.

Nick assumed, however, that the miner would first telephone downstairs. The din would make it difficult for him to be understood, though; and even if he were, he would doubtless grow impatient at the delay and soon leave his room to complain in person to the clerk.

The fact that he was already dressed would make that easy, and Nick counted on his doing so sooner or later. At any rate, he had arranged with Stickney that the bell should continue its exasperating dinning if possible until Stone had been routed out.

On the other hand, there was a possibility, of course, that the man would not act in accordance with expectations. He might remain at the telephone, or even demolish the bell in his anger, especially as he would doubtless be afraid that it would arouse Crawford, and that the latter might not fall asleep again for some time. Nick had to run that risk, though; and now he was impatiently awaiting some sign that his ruse was working as he wished.

The muffled ringing of the bell prevented him from telling whether Stone was telephoning or not, but he had no doubt that such was the case. Would the man stop at that, though?

Evidently not; for two or three minutes after the bell began to ring he caught the sound of an opening door, despite the racket, and almost immediately afterward hurried footsteps passed his room.

He waited for nothing more, but crawled through his window near to the neighboring platform of the fire escape and laid hands on Stone's sash. It came up easily, and revealed an empty room, and the door ajar. It was a risky undertaking, and one that was full of uncertainties. The irate miner might return at any moment. Crawford might come in from the adjoining room and denounce him as a suspicious character, or some one else might put in an appearance to investigate the noise which must have been disturbing many by that time. Worst of all, Stone had left the door partly open and the light on, so that Nick had to work in the open, with a possibility of being seen and interrupted at any moment.

None of these things seemed to worry him, though. He slipped cautiously into the room and looked about him with keen eyes. A faint ejaculation of satisfaction escaped his lips as he caught sight of what he was looking for.

There was a small writing desk close to the head of the bed. It was open, and on the extended leaf lay a small, flat, leather case. Leaping forward, Nick opened the case and took out a small hypodermic syringe. The plunger had been drawn back to its fullest extent, and the detective's lips tightened as he realized that in that little cylinder lurked sure death.

He paid no attention to the other articles in the case—the tiny bottle with some colorless drug, the bit of sponge, and so on. He cared nothing for them, and was interested only in the deadly hypodermic.

Looking about him again, and listening all the while, he took out his fountain pen, removed the cap, and unscrewed the pen itself; then he squirted the contents of the syringe into the barrel of the pen, which he had taken the precaution to empty before leaving his room, and replaced the pen and cap.

Having finished that manipulation, he carelessly thrust the pen back into his pocket and went with long, silent strides to a stationary washstand in a little alcove. He turned on the faucets, directed a little stream of warm water into the syringe, and operated the plunger several times, in order to clean the cylinder as well as he could; after which he filled the syringe with water, and, leaving the plunger out as he had found it, returned the instrument to the case. The case closed, he made for the window.

So swift had been his movements that he had been in the room hardly more than a minute, and nothing had occurred to disturb him. The bell had continued its deafening ringing, and he had thought he heard Crawford's bed creak, but Stone's partner had not called out. He gave a sigh of relief as he reached the balcony of the fire escape and plunged out into the shadows at one side. In a few brief moments he was over the railing and through his own window.

He had hardly reached his room, however, before he heard Stone's familiar footsteps in the corridor outside. The miner was returning, and muttering angrily to himself as he did so. Presently the noise ceased. The bell had been "fixed." The detective heard Stone pass again and yet again, probably to tell the floor clerk that it was all right.

Not until Stone's door was finally closed and locked did the detective drop into a chair. "Whew!" he said, half aloud, "that was warm work, and not very good for the nerves. I've saved Crawford for the time being, but my work isn't done by any means—even for to-night."

He looked at his watch and found that it was quarter past one. There was still an hour and a quarter if Stone obeyed instructions, and Nick had no doubt that he would now. In fact, he might even wait longer, for he would be certain to fear that the ringing of the bell had disturbed Crawford, and would wish to give him plenty of time to fall into a deep sleep again.

Nick did not intend to remain idle, but he felt sure that he had some time to kill, and he was glad of it. Despite his iron nerve, he felt just a trifle shaken by the exacting ordeal through which he had just gone; therefore, he took out a cigar, lighted it, and leaned back in a Morris chair. He must have dozed off before long, for the next thing he knew he sat up with a start. It was half past two.

"Stone will probably be making a move now," he thought, on the alert at once. "I'm glad my mental alarm clock woke me when it did."

CHAPTER XXIV.

THE PLUNGER REACHES HOME.

Once more Nick Carter eased himself out of his window. It was getting to be a habit with him. His long legs bridged the gap as before, but this time his errand was, if possible, even more fraught with risk than the previous ones had been.

He lowered himself over the rail slowly and with infinite care, and then, stooping, crept along the platform to Stone's window. By peering in through the crack between the sill and the partly lowered sash, he saw the tall miner in the act of picking up the little leather case from the writing desk. Stone's back was turned to the detective, and the latter seized the opportunity to slip noiselessly past the window.

A few feet ahead of him loomed another window, dark and open at top and bottom. Winthrop Crawford was fond of fresh air. The lower sash was raised about eighteen inches, which made it possible for Nick to flatten himself over the sill and crawl through. It required daring under the circumstances, but his performance that night would have established a reputation for that sort of thing on the part of any one.

The room was in darkness, but the detective had previously found opportunity to study the position of the furniture. He was able, therefore, to avoid a collision, and his stockinged feet trod softly on the thick carpet. A private bathroom opened off from the bedroom on the side opposite the connecting door which led to Stone's quarters. Nick darted into this and began cautiously to close the door.

"Let's hope our friend Crawford is a sound sleeper," he thought; "and that this door isn't inclined to squeak. If he wakes up now and starts on a burglar hunt, it will mess things up hopelessly."

Crawford's heavy breathing went on uninterruptedly, however, and the sound was reassuring. It seemed to indicate, on the other hand, that Crawford would fall an easy victim to his old partner's attack; but the detective had already pulled Stone's fangs.

He waited perhaps five minutes, standing behind the bathroom door, which he had left slightly ajar. At the end of that time the opposite door, that leading from Stone's room, quietly opened. As it did so, it revealed the fact that Stone had put out his own lights. Nick stiffened, for he knew that the crucial moment was close at hand.

He had taken the risk of entering Crawford's room and secreting himself there partly to witness whatever might happen, and partly because he was by no means sure of James Stone. One never can be certain of what a madman may do. Stone had been supplied with the instruments necessary for the commission of a highly scientific crime, but when the time came, he might discard them, owing to his unfamiliarity with such things, and resort to some more commonplace weapon. In fact, if he made a slip, or if Crawford awoke prematurely and showed fight, it was almost certain that Stone would try to make us of some more familiar way of getting rid of enemies—or supposed enemies. Consequently Nick wanted to be on hand to give instant aid, if necessary. He did not consider that his duty to Crawford had been discharged when he had substituted water for the mysterious and deadly charge which Doctor Follansbee had originally placed in the hypodermic syringe.

Stone came in noiselessly, and the subdued light from the corridor which shone in through the transom accentuated his lean, angular form as it entered. The door was closed carefully behind him, and Nick could hear his suppressed, nervous breathing as he crossed toward the bed.

The intruder paused there within a yard or so of the outstretched form of Crawford, and Nick braced himself in anticipation of a possible emergency. He saw Stone looking toward the bed with his head thrust slightly forward, as if he were listening to Crawford's breathing. Seemingly the man soon became satisfied that all was well, for he took from his pocket a couple of small objects which the detective guessed to be the little vial and sponge.

Stone's movements indicated that he was emptying the contents of the vial into the sponge. As he did so, he took a quick step forward and bent over the bed. Simultaneously there was a stir, and the springs of the bed creaked.

Nick peered out and saw the head and shoulders of Crawford rising from the pillow. The bearded face of the kindly mine owner peered for a moment through the gloom at the vague form bending over him, then a single word came to the detective's ears:

"Jimmy!"

A savage cry sounded, and, with a last bound, the demented partner had thrown himself upon Crawford. Nick heard a choking gasp, and for a moment was tempted to leap from his hiding place and hurl himself upon the would-be murderer. It was only with a supreme effort of will that he kept himself in hand and mutely watched the struggle.

Stone had all the strength of his madness behind him, and with remorseless force he pressed Crawford back upon the pillow. Then, with a quick swoop, he pressed the sponge over the bearded lips and nostrils of the man who loved him better than a brother. There was a convulsive movement of the prone figure, and a long-drawn sigh, then Crawford's arms fell back from their hold on Stone's shoulders and he relapsed into unconsciousness.

Stone's heavy breathing was very audible to the detective as the latter stood watching the dramatic scene. He saw the miner take the little leather case from his pocket and remove the hypodermic syringe. After that, leaning over his unconscious partner, the madman plunged the needle into Crawford's forearm, close to the elbow, and the plunger was pressed home with one quick movement of the powerful thumb.

As soon as the deed was done, Stone gave an exultant exclamation, and, still leaning over the bed, shook his clenched fists at the motionless body.

"It was either you or me, curse you!" he said, as if growling, his face working savagely. "And I have won. You're as good as done for, and unless you stop playing with me as a cat plays with a mouse, you won't have a chance to do what you want to do with me. I've taken care of myself so far, and I guess I can keep on doing it until you're too sick to try any tricks on me. Follansbee says you'll be dead before the twenty-seventh, and he ought to know. Anyway, he won't get his money if you're not."

CHAPTER XXV.
THE MADMAN'S GET-AWAY.

The words were spoken aloud in a thick, jerky voice, and it seemed to be all that Stone could do to keep his clutching hands from his senseless partner's throat. Doubtless he remembered the rascally doctor's promise that Crawford would know nothing about it all when he woke in the morning, and that was probably what stayed his hand.

Had the detective been in any doubt of the man's condition, it would have vanished then, and Stone's irresponsibility was even more evident when he turned away from the bed, and the light from the transom struck his face. It was wrinkled into a mask of maniacal triumph, and the glare in the eyes was more like that of a wild animal than of a human being.

Nick held his breath for a moment. Stone was heading directly toward the bathroom, apparently with the idea of washing his hands after handling the drugged sponge. If he should enter there, discovery would be inevitable, and the detective would have a crazy man to handle—a task which even he did not care to contemplate.

Presently, however, when Stone was only four or five feet from the door of the bathroom, he suddenly wheeled about and recrossed to his own door, through which he disappeared. His shrewdness had evidently suggested the desirability of performing the necessary ablutions in his own room.

Nick relaxed when the danger was removed, and after waiting for perhaps five minutes following the closing of the connecting door, he stole from his hiding place and sought Crawford's bed. No odor of the drug had reached his nostrils in the bathroom. It was evidently so volatile that it had been quickly dissipated in the air. The detective knew its nature, however, for he had sniffed at it in Stone's room. He was aware that it was all that Doctor Follansbee had claimed for it, and that, under ordinary circumstances, it would work no permanent harm; but what he did not know was its effect on Winthrop Crawford. Crawford seemed to possess a rugged constitution, but his heart, for instance, might be weak. Nick wished to make sure that his new friend's condition was normal before he left the room.

His examination, for which he did not need a light, was satisfactory. The drug had plunged Crawford into a profound sleep, but there was nothing to indicate that the effects would not pass away in good time, leaving him in his usual health. As for the injection, that meant nothing, so long as the serum which Follansbee had provided was now reposing in Nick's fountain pen. To be sure, the hasty cleaning of the syringe might not have removed all traces of the serum, but the detective had done his best, and knew enough of such things to feel sure that the consequences, if any, would not be serious. Crawford might possibly have a slight touch of the disease, whatever it was, but it was not likely to amount to much.

The detective straightened up a little, listened, then produced his pocket flash light and turned the rays on Crawford. It was an easy matter to find where the puncture had been made, for a tiny globule of blood stood out on the tanned skin of the man's arm. Nick stooped lower and took a bit of the flesh between thumb and finger. He succeeded in squeezing out a few drops of water and blood, which he carefully wiped away.

"You're safe enough, my friend," he thought. "Anyhow, I've done my best for you, and to-morrow will decide whether you're still foolish enough to refuse to guard yourself against the attacks of that madman, or whether you're willing to listen to reason and let me put him where he belongs."

Having done all he could for the time being, he straightened up and stood in thought for perhaps half a minute, uncertain of his next move. He had heard enough of the conversation between Stone and Follansbee to know that the latter had planned for the miner to join him after the diabolical injection had been made. That meant that Stone would soon venture forth again, doubtless by way of the fire escape, and there was no knowing what moment he might appear at his window. Consequently it would be extra hazardous for Nick to venture out on the platform and try to pass Stone's room.

He decided to wait for a few minutes, and to return to the bathroom to do so, for Stone might take it into his head to come back into Crawford's room for some reason.

In a short time he had the satisfaction of hearing Stone's window go up and then down again after the man had passed through. His alert ears caught a few slight sounds on the fire escape, which told him that the miner had begun to descend. He had planned to follow, if possible, owing to his realization that Follansbee might be playing a double game, and was quite capable of making away with Stone as well as Crawford. He had brought along his shoes for that purpose, having suspended them about his neck by means of the laces, and during the last few minutes he had put them on in the bathroom.

It occurred to him now, though, that the difficulties were even greater than he had looked for. It would not do for the floor clerk to see him emerging from Crawford's room, for she would naturally become suspicious at once, and, not knowing his identity, would cause a delay before an explanation could be made. On the other hand, he could not follow down the fire escape until Stone had disappeared from the courtyard, and by the time he could reach the near-by bank, where Follansbee was to be waiting, the car would doubtless have carried the two conspirators off.

Moreover, he had known all the time that there was small chance of following the machine at that hour. He certainly could not do so on foot, and even if he had arranged for another car to be in waiting in the neighborhood, there would be considerable delay in reaching it. On the whole, therefore, he reluctantly decided to return to his own room, and call it a night's work. It was not that he trusted Follansbee any more, but merely that he thought a few hours' delay would not entail serious consequences to James Stone.

He did not dream, however, of what was in store for the ex-miner.

CHAPTER XXVI.

THE AWAKENING OF REMORSE.

"Have you done the trick?"

Stone dropped back on the soft cushions of the car and passed his hands across his eyes. It had been a hasty and disordered flight that had followed his act, and had carried him down the fire escape. On reaching the lower platform, he had crawled through the ladder opening and let himself down and dropped to the pavement of the court. Then he had sped across the courtyard and out into the side street. There he had moderated his pace for fear of attracting attention, if a passing policeman should see him. He had still hurried along, however, blindly and fearfully, until he saw the waiting machine.

Follansbee's head had been thrust out of the closed car for a moment as Stone approached, then the door had been opened, and the miner had jumped in.

"Where is the syringe?" Follansbee asked.

Stone mechanically thrust his hand into his pocket and withdrew the leather case. There was a look of satisfaction in the physician's eyes as he took charge of his property again.

"I was worried for fear you might have left that behind," he said, in his thin voice. "The most careful of us make slips now and then."

"I made no slip," came the answer, in a strange voice. "If that thing was charged with death as you told me, then Winthrop Crawford is doomed."

"You need have no fear of the potency of my preparation," Follansbee assured him. "From to-night you may look upon yourself as virtually a millionaire."

"I don't care so much about that," the miner began. "It was— —"

His tall, raw-boned form stiffened suddenly, and he drew in a deep, noisy breath—just such a breath as a man might take when awakened from a long sleep. He turned swiftly upon the astonished Follansbee, and the latter involuntarily shrank away. He feared that Stone might do him some harm, and knew that he was far from a physical match for the hard-muscled miner.

Nothing was further from Stone's thoughts, though. His unexpected move had another meaning. "What was it that made me want to kill my best friend?" he demanded, in tragic bewilderment.

Quick as a flash the truth burst on Doctor Follansbee. The strain and intense excitement under which Stone had labored must have wrought a startling but by no means unprecedented change in his mental condition. He was indeed a sleeper awakened. It had probably been some subtle excitement that had unhinged his brain in the first place, and now, thanks to the law of balance, a more powerful excitement had come near to bringing him back to his senses.

"What was it? What was it?" the poor fellow gasped, leaning forward and peering at Follansbee through the half gloom of the limousine. "Why did I want to kill Win? By heavens, man, speak—speak! There must have been a reason!"

The strained voice rose almost to a shriek, and Follansbee began to fear that his companion might attract attention and call down a demand to stop the car for an investigation. Although it was past three o'clock in the morning, the streets were not quite empty, for New York's streets rarely are. They flashed past a brightly lighted corner, and the doctor saw the uniformed figure of a policeman pacing slowly along and looking in their direction. At any moment Stone might burst out into a storm of self-reproach, and there was no telling to what lengths his remorse might carry him. It was a situation which required a master hand, and the way in which Follansbee tackled it was typical of his shrewdness and lack of conscience.

Instead of attempting to explain to Stone, he leaned forward suddenly and gave the miner a hearty clap on the shoulder.

"At last!" he ejaculated, in tones of the greatest relief and satisfaction. "Thank Heaven you've come back to your senses."

He was playing a deep game now, and the way in which the haggard eyes of his companion turned upon him might have touched his heart had anything been there to touch.

"Come back to my senses!" Stone repeated uncomprehendingly. "What do you mean by that?"

Then a great hope flamed up in his eyes. Had Follansbee been merely humoring him, seeming to fall in with his madness? Had the hypodermic been harmless after all?

CHAPTER XXVII.
AN ASTOUNDING STATEMENT.

James Stone's questions, both uttered and unexpressed, were not to be answered just then. A sudden swerve of the car made Follansbee look out of the window. The machine had turned into Amsterdam Avenue, and a few moments later had come to a halt before the physician's door.

A ragged, shuffling figure, that of a hollow-cheeked young man, was passing at the moment. The young fellow, apparently a homeless vagrant, or worse, paused as the car drew up to the curb, then darted forward and opened the door.

Doctor Follansbee muttered something under his breath, seemingly derogatory to the volunteer, and he and Stone crossed the pavement and vanished through the doorway while the car went on up the street.

Apparently disgusted by his bad luck in not obtaining a tip, the disreputable-looking young man crossed the street and disappeared into the shadows of an areaway, which primitive lodging place seemed to be his choice for the night.

Meanwhile, Follansbee had unlocked the door with his latchkey, switched on the lights in the hall and office, and motioned his companion to enter the latter. The lights shone brightly on the former mine owner's face, and the doctor was almost startled by the change in it. The hard, sour, brooding expression that had so characterized the tanned features had vanished now, and in its place was a very sane anxiety, coupled with shocked recollection. James Stone was plainly suffering in a way that few men are called upon to suffer. "Now," he said at once, refusing the proffered chair, "tell me what you mean."

Even his voice had subtly changed. It was still deep, but the hoarseness had gone from it, and it had taken on a little of the mellowness of Crawford's own.

Follansbee advanced to his desk and dropped into a chair.

"Won't you sit down?" he repeated, with perfect self-possession. "It's a rather long story."

"No, no! I would rather stand," Stone replied, pressing his hand to his brow. "I feel dazed and sick; I feel as though a great gap had come into my life, and that I was only returning to the world again after a long absence."

He stared down at Follansbee with anguished eyes.

"Everything—or nearly everything—is misty," he went on, "but I know that I came to you on the recommendation of young Doctor Floyd down in Brazil. He sent me to you to get help for my trouble, but—but somehow, instead of that, we hatched a devilish plot to murder the best friend I have in the world, Win Crawford. In Heaven's name what's to be done? What did you mean just now when you said I had come to my senses? I have come to them, I hope, but if it's too late to help Win, I would have been far better off as I was. If he dies now, I shall kill myself. I could not bear to live knowing that I had murdered him. You don't know—nobody knows—how much he has meant to me. Tell me, man, what you meant? Is there—is there any hope?"

His terrible anxiety was pathetic to see, but it seemed to have no effect on Stephen Follansbee. The latter looked on as if he were witnessing a play, and as soon as Stone paused, his cold voice cut like a knife through the silence.

"For a considerable period, Mr. Stone—several months, I understand—your mind has been seriously affected in certain respects," he said. "Perhaps I should say that it has been affected in one particular respect. A few days ago you came to me and seemed to jump to the conclusion that I was the archfiend himself, or something little better. If you had been sane, I would have thrown you out of the house for your insults. As it was, I listened to you and led you on until you made an extraordinary proposal; nothing less than that I should help you to put your partner out of the way. Frankly I came very near to using the telephone then and there, and having you placed in custody."

"I wish now you had!" Stone burst out.

He was laboring under the greatest excitement and remorse, but he was obviously as sane as he had ever been in his life.

"I did not do so, however," Follansbee went on, ignoring the interruption, "for I saw that your trouble was monomania; serious enough in itself, but leaving you sane in all other ways. I diagnosed it also as a mere temporary derangement, and I did not feel justified in submitting you to the ordeal of publicity, or of committing you to an asylum."

"Go on! Be quick about it! What did you do? For Heaven's sake tell me the whole thing at once!"

Follansbee slipped his hand into the inside breast pocket of his coat and drew out a little leather case.

"I simply played a professional trick on you, Mr. Stone," he declared quietly. "It's true that the drug in the vial was a powerful narcotic, and at this very moment I have no doubt that your friend is still under the influence of it."

As he spoke, he opened the case and took out the syringe.

"But this," he went on, tapping the instrument, "was charged with nothing more harmful than pure glycerine."

"Is that true?" the miner demanded, striding forward and towering above the diminutive specialist. "If it is——"

"I can easily convince you that it is," Follansbee assured him.

He unfastened his cuff link and pulled up his cuff, revealing a lean, yellow forearm.

"Watch!" he said.

CHAPTER XXVIII.

"YOU'VE SAVED ME FROM MYSELF!"

"You probably did not inject all of it," Follansbee continued, as he withdrew the plunger of the syringe.

He thrust the needle beneath the skin of his arm and pressed the plunger almost home; then, as he withdrew the syringe, a tiny drop of clear liquid appeared on the end of the needle, and a further compression of the plunger caused the globule to drop on his arm under the puncture.

"There, that ought to convince any man, sane or insane," the cool voice resumed. "Had this been a deadly culture, you will admit that I would hardly be so mad as to run even the slightest risk of being infected by it."

His manner and act carried conviction to the perturbed brain of James Stone.

There was a chair close to the desk, and the tall figure collapsed into it. Stone stretched his arms out across the desk, dropped his head between them, and gave vent to a hoarse sob.

"Thank Heaven! Oh, thank Heaven!" he said, in a choked voice. "I've been in torment these last few months, but it was all for the best. You've saved me from myself, doctor, and I don't know how to thank you!"

The hawklike face above him creased with satisfaction, and the thin lips curled back from the sharp teeth.

"I ask no thanks," was the reply. "And allow me to remind you that I hold your check for a substantial sum. That is the best thanks to a man who needs all the money he can lay hands on in order to carry on costly experiments. I trust you will not regret having given it to me, although you did so under a misapprehension. You'll remember, however, that I did not promise, at that time, to do away with Crawford. I merely promised that he would not trouble you after the twenty-seventh, and I have kept to the agreement. He will not trouble you, because all your differences will have vanished by that time—have vanished now, in fact. Later, of course, I felt compelled to fall in more nearly with your misguided desires, but that was nothing more than professional tact. If you had called yourself the King of Mexico, I would have humored you in that belief, and bowed down to you."

"I understand, of course—now," Stone replied gravely. "As for your fee, it's by no means too much for what you've done. Your skill has given me back my sanity and my old friend. Say nothing more about it."

Follansbee was not looking to drop the subject, however.

"I won't after this," he said, "but that reminds me that the check is for a rather large amount, and it has occurred to me that your bank may make some difficulty about cashing it. I won't present it before Monday, the twenty-seventh, of course, but if you would write a note to the bank now, it might help matters."

Gratitude and relief made James Stone less cautious than he might otherwise have been. "Certainly," he said, without hesitation. "I'll be glad to do so."

"Thank you. I think I have some of your hotel stationery here in my pocket. Yes, here it is. I remember picking some up in the writing room the other day when I was waiting for you, and wished to make some notes."

He produced several sheets of paper engraved with the name of the Hotel Windermere, and, selecting one of them, spread it out on the desk before his visitor.

His explanation of the possession of the paper was sufficiently plausible, and Stone was not in a critical mood. The result was that the miner scrawled a brief letter of introduction for Follansbee, accompanied with a request that the check be cashed without question.

If he had only ventured to look up as he signed the note, he might have been warned that all was not well, but he did not think of doing so. Follansbee rose to his feet, and, taking the letter, slipped it into a plain envelope. Evidently he had not thought best to provide a hotel envelope in addition to the paper, for that thorough preparation might have seemed a little suspicious.

"And now," he said, "before you go, I'd like to offer you a little refreshment, if I may. I have some very good brandy, and a bit of it would tone you up. You need it after all you've gone through to-night. After that you can go back to the hotel."

He did not know that Nick's ruse in regard to the bell had spoiled Stone's alibi. Had he been aware of the fact, it would have given him much food for thought, but it would not have affected his words to Stone, for they were spoken merely for effect.

"And in the morning," he added, "you will find Mr. Crawford as well as he ever was in his life."

"You are sure of that?" Stone asked eagerly. "The drug can't possibly do him any permanent harm?"

"On my professional honor, it cannot," Follansbee assured him. "He won't know anything about it when you see him again."

He had reached the sideboard now, and he picked up two glasses which stood beside the decanter containing the brandy. Stone was by his side as he poured the liquor, but the ex-miner did not see a suspicious move. Perhaps it was because he was not in a suspicious mood. At any rate, there can be no doubt that it was something more than brandy that he drank.

Little more than five minutes later Doctor Follansbee accompanied Stone to the door, shook hands with him, and watched him depart. Stone had suggested the use of the doctor's phone to call a taxi, but Follansbee had advised against it.

"If you're wise, you'll walk; at least, a part of the way," he had said. "You've been through a great deal to-night, and the exercise will be good for you. If you can get physically tired, so much the better. You'll be more apt to sleep when you reach your room."

Stone had taken the advice, and started off on foot. After lingering at the door for a few minutes, the specialist closed it and disappeared into the house. Very shortly the lights went out, and he reappeared on the steps.

Seemingly, he, too, was going for a stroll, although it was nearly four o'clock in the morning by that time.

Curiously enough, Follansbee headed in the same direction which Stone had taken, and, more curious still, a slouching figure emerged from an areaway, crossed the street, and flitted along behind the head physician of St. Swithin's.

The night had been full enough, but it looked as if other things were still to be crammed into it.

CHAPTER XXIX.

A STRANGE DEVELOPMENT.

Doctor Stephen Follansbee walked along at a slow pace, but his movements were not characteristic. His hands were not folded behind him, and his head was erect, as if he were peering into the distance in front, instead of casting his eyes on the ground as he usually did.

He had walked down Amsterdam Avenue for several blocks when a faint monosyllable issued from his lips.

"Ah!" he murmured, and sightly quickened his pace.

The young man who was keeping him in sight from the other side of the street—and who was evidently the same one who had opened the limousine door some time earlier—could not hear the ejaculation, but he noted the quickened steps and glanced ahead in search of a reason.

Half a block beyond was a little group of men gathered on the sidewalk. When Follansbee approached, he found that it consisted of a couple of policemen, and the driver of a taxicab was bending over the figure of a tall man lying prone on the sidewalk. The physician had no need to do more than glance at the figure, for, as the policeman lifted the body, the rigid features of James Stone were revealed.

Clearing his throat, Follansbee stepped forward. "What's the trouble, officer?" he asked. "Has there been any accident?"

One of the men in uniform turned and looked at Follansbee in a questioning way.

"I'm Doctor Stephen Follansbee, of St. Swithin's Hospital," the specialist went on. "Here's my card. If I can help you in any way, I shall be only too glad to do so."

The patrolman took the card and glanced at it in the light of a near-by street lamp. When he saw the name and the string of letters after it, his attitude instantly changed to one of great respect. It was a name to conjure with in New York City.

"It's lucky you happened along, Doctor Follansbee," the spokesman declared, making way for the newcomer, who stooped and seemed to make an examination.

"It seems to be a paralytic stroke," Follansbee announced presently. "You had better call an ambulance and have him taken somewhere at once." Then, as if struck by a new idea, he went on: "Come to think of it, you might as well send him to St. Swithin's. I was going there in a few minutes, anyway. There's a special case that needs watching. Why not put him in this taxi?"

The cool cunning of the man had its reward.

Under ordinary circumstances, the unfortunate Stone would have been taken to another hospital—one with an emergency ward—but at Follansbee's suggestion the inert, heavily-breathing form was lifted into the machine, and one of the policeman took his place beside it. Up Amsterdam Avenue, toward the big hospital over which Follansbee presided, the cab made its way. Follansbee himself had climbed into the seat beside the driver, and the ragged young man who had been following him looked uncertainly after the dwindling vehicle.

From that the vagrant's gaze shifted to the remaining policeman, who was eying him suspiciously.

"This is no place for me," thought the young fellow; and he made off hurriedly along the side street before the officer had time to accost him.

It was Patsy Garvan, Nick Carter's second assistant, and he was doing an almost unheard-of thing. In other words, he was there without his chief's knowledge or sanction. It was not as much of a breach of discipline as it might have been, however, for he was under Chick's orders. Chick had something of a grudge against Doctor Follansbee, and had not been altogether satisfied with his chief's assurance that he should have a hand in the case later on. It was impossible for him to do anything himself, because he was in charge at the detective's headquarters in the absence of Carter; but he had done the next best thing. He had found no trouble in inducing Patsy Garvan to shadow Follansbee's house while Nick Carter was watching James Stone at the hotel.

"Follansbee is a slippery customer," Chick had confided to the other, "and it strikes me that he needs a little attention. He's capable of almost anything, and I'd like nothing better than to bring him up short without the chief's help. As that's out of the question, though, I'm going to turn him over to you. Don't let the chief know what you're up to, if you can help it. I'd like to surprise him with some information that would be news to him; and when it comes to a showdown, I'll take all the responsibility."

Patsy had accepted the added task with his usual promptness, and had been leading a sort of double life for several days. During the hours of daylight he went about his regular duties as usual. As it happened, Nick did not give him much night work; consequently he was able to shadow Follansbee's house night after night. He had enjoyed little sleep, but he did not seem to mind that. He, too, was convinced that Follansbee was an unusually dangerous man, and should be carefully "covered," and he was more than willing to do the job.

Now his feelings were decidedly mixed. He had ventured to mingle with the group about the prostrate man, and had discovered his identity. It was unquestionably James Stone, the man he had seen entering Follansbee's house a short time before, and had subsequently left it.

Patsy had seen Follansbee watching Stone as the latter started down the street, and he knew that the doctor had deliberately waited a few minutes, and then followed. This meant that the scoundrelly head of St. Swithin's had looked for Stone to succumb on the street, and had planned to have it appear as if by accident.

"This is a queer go," thought Patsy as he hurried away from the neighborhood of the curious policeman. "Follansbee must have double crossed Stone just as Patsy feared he might, and it was pretty foxy of him to have arranged that the man should take a tumble on the street several blocks from his house.

"I've stumbled over a discovery sure enough, and now it's up to me to report to Chick and let him tell the chief, as I suppose he will. It might have been well for me to trail that taxi in order to make sure of its destination, but I don't believe there can be any doubt about that. Follansbee suggested St. Swithin's, and the policeman who went along would want to know the why and wherefore of any change in plan. It seems safe enough to assume, therefore, that the Buzzard is taking his latest victim to St. Swithin's, and that's enough for the present. I'd like to know what the mischief he's up to, and what he expects to do with him at the hospital, but that will have to keep. Thank Fortune I was on hand to-night. I'll bet the chief didn't dream that this little affair was going to be pulled off; if not, he certainly ought to thank Chick and me for giving him the tip."

CHAPTER XXX.

AN UNLUCKY MORNING.

Patsy Garvan had reason to congratulate himself on the outcome of his night's vigil, but it is to be feared that he did not follow it up in the best way. It was nearly half past four in the morning when he reached Nick's headquarters, and he unwisely decided that there was no use of rousing Chick at that hour. Breakfast was only about three hours off, and he reasoned that the delay could make little difference.

Whatever Follansbee had done to Stone was an accomplished fact, and it was not likely that any more serious steps would be taken that night. Besides, St. Swithin's Hospital was not an easy place to commit a crime, even though the criminal was at the head of it. If Follansbee meant to murder Stone, and had drugged him to get him into his power, the murder would probably be a slow and subtle one. In that case a few hours were unimportant.

Consequently Patsy made his way quietly to his own room without rousing Chick or leaving any word for him. He removed his make-up, slipped out of his ragged suit with a sigh of relief, and was asleep almost as soon as he touched the bed. He fully expected to be up again by half past seven at the latest, and counted on being called if he showed any tendency to oversleep. He did not realize, however, that he had had very little rest for several days, and that Nature would do her best to make up the shortage as soon as she had the chance. Nor did it occur to him that Chick, knowing that he had been doing double duty, might give orders not to have him called if he did not appear for breakfast on time.

The result was that when he awakened, it was to discover that the sun was pouring into his room with a warmth and intensity which proved that the day was several hours old. He rose up in bed with a start and looked at the little clock on the table.

"Half past eleven!" he ejaculated, in amazement. "Great Scott! I wouldn't have had this happen for the world. Why the dickens didn't I make a report of some sort last night before turning in? I might have known that I would sleep like a log, and that Chick might see I wasn't disturbed."

Without stopping to dress, he stuck his head out of the door and shouted Chick's name at the top of his voice. The housekeeper heard him, and came bustling down the hall.

"Mr. Chick was called out of town this morning," she said, greatly to the young assistant's chagrin.

"Where to?" he demanded.

"To Providence."

"To a hotel?"

"I'll bring you the note he left for Mr. Carter."

She hurried into the celebrated detective's study and presently returned with a slip of paper. On it the chief assistant had explained his errand, and said that he hoped to be back by night, but would be running about most of the day. He added that he would try to keep in touch with the Sound Hotel, and could be reached there if he was wanted.

The information did not sound promising, but Patsy was obliged to make the best of it. Putting on a bath robe and slippers, he ran to the chief's study and attempted to reach Chick on the long-distance telephone. As he had anticipated, he had not yet arrived at the hotel. He left a message asking that he be called as soon as possible; but after he had done so, he decided that he could not wait for that. There were too many uncertainties, and the delay might prove serious.

"Confound it, this is a pretty mess," he told himself. "I can't be sure about Chick any more. I'll have to 'fess up to the chief—if I can get hold of him."

The housekeeper was once more summoned, and from her Patsy learned that the chief had not been there either the night before or that morning.

"He's still at the Windermere, I suppose," the housekeeper suggested.

"Let's hope he is," Patsy answered, and returned to the phone. He gave the number of the Hotel Windermere, and was promptly connected.

"Is Mr. Mortimer—Mr. Thomas Mortimer—there?" he inquired anxiously.

"One moment, please."

He kept the receiver to his ear for a few seconds, and then the clerk's voice sounded again.

"Hello?" it said. "Mr. Mortimer isn't in at present. He went out with a friend immediately after breakfast. He's been gone about two hours now."

Patsy could have kicked himself at that moment. "Have you any idea where he has gone?"

"No, I haven't. He went out with another of our guests, though, and——"

The assistant caught eagerly at that clew. "Was it Mr. Crawford?" he asked.

"Yes, that's the gentleman. I'm sorry I can't tell you more. Mr. Mortimer doesn't seem to have left any word. Will you leave a message for him?"

Patsy thought for a moment. "No, I believe not," he said, after a pause. "I'll telephone later on, or drop around there."

He replaced the receiver and leaned back disappointedly. "Worse and more of it," he mused. "First, Chick slips out of my reach, and now the chief is off somewhere. This is certainly my unlucky morning. Of course, Chick didn't suppose I had anything of importance to report, and that's why he let me sleep. Now time is flying. Follansbee has got Stone in his clutches for some beastly purpose of his own, and I don't know what to do about it. It's up to the chief to decide that, and I can't reach him."

He had not dictated a message for Carter because the matter was too confidential for that; besides, he expected to present himself at the hotel before long and wait for his chief, if the latter had not yet returned.

First, though, he must dress and snatch a bite of breakfast. His dressing and shaving occupied only about twenty minutes in all—with a cold plunge thrown in—and when he reached the dining room, he found the housekeeper waiting for him. His coming seemed to be a signal, for she vanished at once into the regions behind, but soon returned bearing a tray. Patsy was a favorite of hers, and she was doing him the honor of serving him in person.

"Mr. Chick said to let you sleep," she declared, nodding her gray head. "Heaven only knows when you came in last night. I was awake until twelve."

Patsy grinned. "You missed me by a minute or two," he answered, as he attacked his breakfast.

His conscience was pricking him most uncomfortably, and although he was hungry, he would have eaten little if he had had his own way. The housekeeper stood over him, however, and saw to it that he made a good meal. The breakfast consumed fifteen minutes of his precious time, and even then the elderly lady sniffed as she picked up the tray.

"You oughtn't to bolt your food like that, Mr. Garvan," she complained. "You'll be a martyr to indigestion before you're forty. Don't you think you might bite a thing twice before it goes down?"

She had gained her main point, however, and that was something. She returned to the kitchen, and Patsy hurried out of the house.

He had ordered one of Nick's runabouts brought round, and in it he drove to the hotel.

"Mr. Mortimer" had not yet returned.

He said something under his breath, and decided not to wait. He was too uneasy by that time, for James Stone's fate was troubling him. Accordingly he left word with the clerk for "Mr. Mortimer" to remain in when he came, if possible, until he could be communicated with. That done, he jumped into the runabout again and headed northward in the direction of St. Swithin's Hospital.

It was well that he did so, for his luck was to change.

CHAPTER XXXI.

NICK HAS A HUNCH.

"You, Carter!"

Winthrop Crawford had raised himself in bed, and, leaning on one arm, was staring wonderingly at the figure of the detective seated in a chair close to the head of the bed.

Nick had removed his false mustache, and although he was still dressed in one of the suits he had worn as "Thomas Mortimer," Crawford recognized the clean-cut features.

"It is rather an early hour to make a call, Crawford," the detective said, with an apologetic smile.

"Oh, I'm always glad to see you," was the answer. "Hanged if I understand how you got in, though. Wasn't my door locked?"

"I believe it was," was the calm response.

"Then ― ―"

"Oh, you ought to know that locked doors don't trouble me, Crawford," Nick broke in, his smile broadening. "I sometimes tickle their keyholes a little, and sometimes pass around them."

He was delighted and greatly relieved to have Crawford awake and evidently in such good trim.

"And which method did you employ in this instance?" inquired the man on the bed, with a twinkle in his eyes.

"I'll tell you all about that when I come to it. It's too long to be dismissed in a sentence. As a matter of fact, this is by no means my first visit to your room since you went to bed last night, and I've spent considerable time here."

Crawford looked bewildered. "What on earth for?" he demanded; then, as he saw Nick eying him queerly, he added: "Why are you looking at me like that? What has happened?"

Instead of answering, the detective put another question. "How do you feel this morning?" he queried.

Crawford searched Nick's face as though he were half afraid that his visitor had lost his senses.

"I feel like a fighting cock," he said promptly. "Why should I feel any other way?"

Nick's face had grown stern. "Because some five or six hours ago," he answered gravely, "you were forcibly drugged, and a murderous attack was made upon you."

The blank look of amazement that came into Crawford's eyes increased as memory returned to him. He sat up in bed and stared at the detective.

"Good heavens, I remember now!" he broke out. "I—I thought at first, though, that it was only a nightmare." He raised his brown, muscular hand and passed it across his brow. "Yes," he muttered slowly, "I remember—I saw Jim Stone—I saw the wet sponge—his terrible face!"

His voice died away into a frail whisper, whereupon Nick came up closer to the bed and laid a kindly hand on the man's shoulder.

"Stone drugged you," he explained; "but that was not the worst he tried to do. The drug was only administered so that you might be kept quiet during what was to follow. Look!"

With a quick movement he pulled back Crawford's right sleeve, and then, extending his finger, indicated a small speck of hardened blood on the tanned forearm.

"That mark covers a puncture made by the hypodermic syringe," the calm voice went on, "and it was charged with the bacilli of some deadly disease when it was first handed to Stone to operate with."

The mine owner listened rigidly.

"Again?" he whispered hoarsely. "Jim has tried again?"

"Yes, and he came very near accomplishing it this time," the detective answered. "Fortunately, however, I was in a position to take a hand. Had I not done so, I'm afraid it would have been all up with you. Neither you nor any one else would have known of what had happened, and by the time you had begun to feel the effects of the injection you would probably have been beyond hope or help."

He seated himself at the foot of the bed and quietly told the whole story. Before it was concluded, the lined, russet face of the miner had become sallow and beaded with perspiration. He leaned back on the pillow, his hands clasped behind his head.

"This is frightful; far more so than anything I dreamed of," he said, in an uncertain voice. "How can I reward you for what you've done?"

The detective leaned forward and laid his hands on the covers over one of the raised knees.

"The only reward I ask for," he said, "is to see you rouse yourself to the true situation. If there was any doubt before, certainly none can be present now. Your old partner is insane, and has fallen into the hands of one of the most cunning, unscrupulous rascals at large to-day. He was dangerous enough before when he only had the shrewdness of his own misguided instincts to aid him, but now you're up against something much worse. You have to deal not only with a homicidal lunatic, but through him with a scientific criminal of the most dangerous sort. The combination is an extraordinary one, and has possibilities for evil that stagger the imagination."

"Do you really believe that—about this doctor, I mean?"

"I'm sure of it. Long before I ever saw you I knew he was a scamp. That's why I took a room here at the Windermere when I found that Stone was consorting with him."

"Is it possible? I don't understand it. Isn't he the one I told you about—the one whom young Floyd recommended to Jimmy?"

"I take it for granted that he is. He has a reputation second to none in his line, and there's no reason to suppose that your own friend was not sincere when he made the condition that Stone should visit Doctor Follansbee. If so, though, he has a great deal to learn about the scoundrelly head of St. Swithin's Hospital."

"But in what way is Follansbee a scoundrel? I should think he would have altogether too much to lose by crime, no matter what his secret tendencies were. What can he hope to gain by using poor Jim's irresponsible enmity to me? He is jeopardizing a great position."

"True, but he thinks he can get away with it," remarked Nick. "They all do, you know—until they wake up. As for his anticipated reward, you may be sure it's a very large one. Follansbee's are always that, and in such a case as this, he must have named a huge price. Stone is in a position, of course, to pay a big sum, and his mental condition makes him an easy victim. That may be the whole explanation, but I have a feeling that it isn't. Something tells me that Follansbee is after more than the fee he has named."

"What are you driving at? How could he profit in any other way by my death?"

"That's what I'd like to find out," Nick told him; "and you ought to be able to help me, if any one can."

"In what way?"

"Well, have you made a will?"

"Yes, I attended to that soon after we sold the Condor."

"And who is the chief beneficiary named in it, may I ask?"

"Jim, of course. He's practically the sole beneficiary, for no other living person has ever been half so close to me as he."

"I shouldn't wonder if that explained it," the detective said thoughtfully.

The bearded mining man looked startled. "I'm afraid I don't follow you," he said. "Tell me plainly what you have in your mind."

"Oh, I may be mistaken," was the answer, "but it seems rather significant. As I've said, your partner's condition makes him an easy mark. Does he by any chance know of the terms of your will?"

"Certainly. I told him what I had done after it was drawn up."

"That's a pity. I do not believe he has his eyes on the money. If I read his mental state aright, he's only actuated by groundless, diseased hate and suspicion, and that so fills his distorted brain that it doesn't leave any room for money considerations. It's very possible, however, that Follansbee has pumped him, and learned the facts in regard to your will. If so, it wouldn't surprise me a bit to find that the rascal was plotting in some way, either with or without Stone's knowledge, to appropriate most, if not all, of your fortune."

"By Jove! I wonder if you're right!"

"I feel that I am. It strikes me that Follansbee wouldn't have taken the risks involved in this thing, especially after having had one brush with me, unless there had been a huge reward in prospect. Half a million or so would tempt almost any man who had any criminal tendencies, you know."

He paused, gazed into vacancy, and then added slowly: "To tell the truth, I'm not convinced that he would be content with your share of the proceeds from the sale of the mine. When the covetousness of a man like that once gets to working, there's no telling to what length it may go. I shouldn't wonder if he aspired to the possession of Stone's share as well as yours."

CHAPTER XXXII.

"THE MAN WHO NEVER LETS GO."

If Winthrop Crawford had been startled before, he was dumfounded now.

"Great guns!" he ejaculated, rising up again and planting his hands on his knees. "Is it possible that you think the fellow is capable of trying to kill Jimmy, too?"

"He's capable of anything, Crawford, if he thinks it is safe. Figure it out for yourself. A demented man comes to him and gets into his power. Follansbee tempts him to unburden himself and makes a criminal proposition. He agrees directly or indirectly to lend the aid of his science for the carrying out of his patient's murderous grudge in return for a substantial fee—twenty-five or fifty thousand dollars, let us say. Incidentally he learns that his patient has been named as the chief beneficiary in the will of the man whose doom is sealed. He naturally itches to get hold of that fortune, or a large part of it, and plots to do so. That's the next step. But there are others—inevitable ones.

"To the best of his knowledge," the detective went on, "his poor, misguided tool carries out his instructions, and inoculates the other man with the active principal of some dread tropical disease. So far, so good—or so bad. What comes next? Why, the logical development, of course. The unscrupulous doctor has schemed in one way or another to benefit by the victim's death, and now when that seems to be provided for, he realizes how completely the man who has actually done the deed is under his thumb.

"His patient is practically a murderer, and, as such, liable to be blackmailed to the limit. Also, the man's brain is unbalanced, and that makes it possible to work upon his fears in an unusual way. Why should such a man have nearly a million in the bank? Can he enjoy it to the full with the specter of remorse always at his elbow? Couldn't somebody else—the doctor, for instance—get a lot more out of that money? The answer is a foregone conclusion; but there's another consideration as well. The doctor has an accomplice whom he cannot trust because of that same mental instability. An insane man is proud of his crimes, and likes to boast about them. He does so without any sense of responsibility. But that would never do in this instance, for such boasting would be almost certain to involve the doctor himself. Therefore, to the latter's mind, there would be an additional reason for getting rid of his patient-accomplice. An additional fortune on the one hand—as a result of a little more clever manipulation—and the prevention of indiscreet blabbing on the other. Can you doubt the outcome?"

Crawford seized Nick's arm excitedly. "You're right!" he agreed. "Jimmy isn't safe for a moment while he's in that fiend's clutches. Where is he now?"

"I don't know," the detective admitted. "He went away with Follansbee after giving you the injection. It was impossible for me to follow at the time; besides, I was altogether too uneasy in mind about you. I realized that your partner might be running into danger, but up to that time it had not come to me so forcibly as it did since. Even if it had, however, I should still have felt that my first duty was to you, and that your safety was more important."

"No, no!" cried the miner, gripping Nick's arm until it ached. "You're wrong there! My life is nothing to me compared with Jimmy's safety. Hasn't he come back yet?"

"I don't think so. He hasn't been in his room, at least."

"Then there isn't a moment to lose. Good heavens, this is maddening! Something terrible may have happened to him. We may be too late."

"Calm yourself," the detective advised kindly. "I don't think you need fear any immediate danger. Follansbee uses subtle methods in order to cover his tracks, and subtle methods take time."

"That may be, but I cannot have a moment's peace until Jimmy is found and wrested from that devil's influence. I'll dress at once, and——"

"Go ahead," Nick interrupted, getting up from the bed. "You mustn't think of taking a hand in this, though."

"But I must, man—for Jimmy's sake. You admit yourself that you let him go off with that rascal without lifting a hand."

"That's true, but if you feel this way about it, I'll consider him first hereafter. You can't take part in it in person, though. I must insist upon your keeping out of it. Remember your position, Crawford. You're supposed to have been infected by that injection, and you're also supposed to know nothing about it. You can't admit any knowledge of the hypodermic without letting the cat out of the bag and putting Follansbee on his guard against me."

"That's true," murmured the miner. "I was forgetting that. What can I do, then?"

"You'll have to keep your hands off and trust me to manage the affair."

"I will, if you'll promise not to have Jimmy locked up, if you can possibly avoid it; and, above all, not to charge him with this latest mad attempt against my life. As I told you before, nobody else is in any danger from him. I'm sure of that, and I'm still willing to take any risk in order to shield him, even after what happened last night. If you can get him away from Follansbee, and put him in the care of some conscientious physician—some one who won't hustle him off to an asylum the first thing—I shall be satisfied."

The detective smiled grimly. "That's all very well," he said; "but what about Follansbee? Don't you realize that if we let one of them off, both will necessarily go free?"

"I suppose so," confessed Crawford. "I'd give anything to see that scoundrel get all that's coming to him, but you understand my position. I can't and won't consent to sacrifice my old partner for the sake of punishing his accomplice. That's out of the question. Follansbee is as dangerous as they make them, I'll admit, but I'm afraid you'll have to find some way of getting around it—of reaching him without involving Stone."

"You make my task a very hard one," Nick told him gravely. "In the face of such a condition, Follansbee seems to be beyond reach; but perhaps he isn't. We'll have to wait and see. He may make a false step before we get through, and if he does——"

He did not finish the sentence, but the way in which he said the words boded no good to Doctor Stephen Follansbee. Crawford had only to look at the detective at that moment to realize why Nick Carter was called "the man who never lets go."

CHAPTER XXXIII.

WILL HE SCORE?

Winthrop Crawford was not satisfied, however. His anxiety was centered about the welfare of his old friend, and he could not lose sight of Stone's continued absence from the Windermere.

"But what are you going to do about Jimmy?" he asked eagerly. "Don't delay, man. Hunt him up as soon as possible, even if you have to defy Follansbee, and mess things up generally in order to do so."

"Don't worry about that, Crawford. I'll look out for your friend. He may have spent the night at Follansbee's house. At any rate, the doctor is a marked man, and if Stone has gone anywhere with his companion, it ought to be a comparatively easy matter to trace them. You can't stay here, though, while I'm doing it."

"Why not?"

"For various reasons. If you did so, and Stone came back, it would be hard to act as if nothing had happened, and he would be watching you with lynx eyes, waiting to see the effect of the injection. I haven't had time yet to analyze the original contents of the syringe, so that I can't say just how the stuff is supposed to act. In order to be on the safe side, though, you'll have to leave the Windermere for the time being. If you're out of their sight, they will not be able to keep tabs on your condition, and we can easily enough make them believe that the disease which they suppose has been introduced into your system is following its normal course."

"But won't Jimmy think it strange if I disappear after I've stuck to him so long—stuck to him against his will?"

"You can leave word for him. Write him a note and make some excuse that will sound plausible."

"Yes, I could do that," the miner agreed. "Where do you want me to go?"

"I haven't thought of any particular place as yet. That will come later, but it is necessary that you should go away at once. Furthermore, I want the people here in the hotel to see you and me go out together."

Crawford soon became convinced that something of the sort was desirable. He was very reluctant to leave the hotel before learning anything definite concerning Stone's whereabouts, but there seemed no help for it, and Nick promised to let him know at frequent intervals whenever anything new came up. By half-past nine o'clock Crawford and the detective—the latter once more in the guise of Thomas Mortimer—were eating their breakfast in the dining room. Making a pretense of eating, however, would be the better way of describing the half-hearted way in which the man from South America toyed with his food.

Before ten o'clock they had both left the Windermere without giving any one a hint as to their destination. So far as the detective knew, he was the only one on the case; therefore it did not occur to him to keep Chick advised of his comings and goings.

Crawford took with him nothing in the way of baggage; therefore they were obliged to purchase a suit case and enough clothing for a few days. That done, they boarded a train at the Grand Central Terminal, and about half an hour later alighted in one of the northern suburbs within sight of Long Island Sound.

A motor bus from the hotel met the train and took them to a huge pile of masonry on a hill overlooking the water. It was one of the best-known hotels in the neighborhood of New York, and much frequented by those who wished to go away from the bustle of the great city for a few days. There Crawford registered, at Nick's suggestion, under an assumed name.

They had parted, and the detective was already descending the steps, when the miner ran after him.

"I've just thought of something that may help you to an understanding of poor old Jim's condition," Crawford said breathlessly. "It has occurred to me that he used to knock about the mine without his hat on last year in all that broiling sun, and I know that many years ago, when he was a boy, an axhead hit him on the skull. He was watching somebody chop wood, and the head became loosened and flew off the handle. Isn't it possible that that injury affected him somehow, but that the trouble didn't manifest itself until recently?"

Nick nodded. "There may be something in that," he said. "The exposure to the sun may have developed the latent disease, somewhat in the way photographic film is developed. I'm glad you told me of that. It makes it clearer than ever that your friend is a victim himself, and should not be judged harshly."

"That's it," Crawford agreed eagerly. "He deserves all the mercy you can show him, Carter. I'm positive that if he ever returns to his senses he will be absolutely heartbroken to hear what he has tried to do. I tell you, Jimmy Stone loves me like a brother, and he would rather cut off his right hand than harm me. You must save him—save him from Follansbee first of all, and then from himself. If you do, there's nothing you can't ask of me."

Nick ignored the generous promise. "The affection of man for man is a wonderful thing, Crawford," he said quietly. "I'm glad to have known you and had this proof of what loyalty means. I must go now, though. Try to have patience and take things as quietly as you can. I'll do my best for Stone, and telephone you from time to time."

As he returned to the station, the detective felt sure that his promise to Winthrop Crawford would greatly hamper his movements but he shrugged his shoulders philosophically.

"Follansbee is a lucky rascal, and a keen one," he thought. "He has remained in the background, and even that telltale conversation I overheard last night doesn't seem destined to be used as a weapon against him. He's certainly stolen a base or two, but he may yet be called out at the home plate!"

CHAPTER XXXIV.

A VISIT TO THE BANK.

The journey to and from the suburban hotel had occupied considerable time, and it was almost one o'clock before the detective returned to the Windermere.

The clerk saw him enter the lobby and called him to the desk. He was informed of the telephone message and of Patsy's call at the hotel. He realized, of course, that one of his assistants had been trying to get in touch with him, but he did not know that it was in connection with that particular case.

Moreover, something came up which made it necessary for him to disregard Patsy's injunction to remain in until he could be reached.

"Mr. Crawford hasn't come back yet, Mr. Mortimer?" the clerk asked. "The gentleman seemed to know him, too."

The detective had turned away from the desk, but he faced about and shook his head.

"I'm afraid that Crawford will not be back for some time," he replied. "He was taken very ill while we were out together, and I had to remove him to a hospital. I'm not quite sure what's the matter with him. I'm afraid, though, that it's some sort of fever which he may have contracted in South America."

The hotel clerk looked startled. "It's nothing very serious, I hope?" he said.

"I trust not," was the reply. "The hospital people feel sure that it isn't contagious, if that's what you mean."

Again he started to leave the desk, but the clerk once more detained him. "A messenger came from the Standard National Bank about half an hour ago," the young man explained. "He asked for either Mr. Stone or Mr. Crawford, and said it was very important. Mr. Stone was in his room in the small hours of the morning, I understand, but he isn't there now, and nobody seems to have seen him about the building this morning."

A little glint came into Nick's eyes, but the clerk did not notice it.

"The Standard National is near here, isn't it?" he inquired, although he knew perfectly well.

"Yes, it's just around the corner," and the clerk indicated the direction.

"Then I think I'll drop around there. I can give them some information about Crawford, anyway; besides, we've come to know each other pretty well."

His manner was careless, but inwardly he attached a great deal of importance to the bit of information which by chance had come his way. It suggested one of the possibilities he had feared, namely, that Follansbee would try some trick to get possession of a large sum of money belonging to one or the other of the partners, or both.

It being Saturday, he found the bank closed when he reached it, but most of the employees were still on hand, and his knock soon brought a response. He mentioned his business to the clerk who opened the door, and a few moments later he was led into the cashier's room. The bank official had expected either Stone or Crawford, and his face betrayed his disappointment. His manner was another proof that something out of the ordinary had occurred, or was impending.

Nick drew a card front his pocket and held it out silently. As soon as the cashier saw the name, "Nicholas Carter," his eyes widened.

"There's nothing wrong, Mr. Carter, I hope?" he asked quickly. "I was very doubtful of honoring the check, but I had Mr. Stone's own note to justify me."

From the desk at his elbow he picked up a sheet of paper bearing the Hotel Windermere heading, and held it out. Nick glanced at the big, careless scrawl.

"Yes," he said. "I've seen specimens of Stone's writing, and I don't think there's any doubt that this is his."

The cashier then extended a check marked "paid," and made out to "S. Follansbee."

There were probably several men among New York City's five millions who had the right to that name and initial, but it seemed perfectly safe to eliminate all but one. It was the sum called for, however, that riveted the detective's attention at once and caused him to fairly gasp.

"Four hundred and fifty thousand dollars!" he ejaculated. "Great Scott! That practically cleans out Stone's account, doesn't it?"

"It leaves only twenty-five or thirty thousand, I believe," was the worried answer.

The detective was still examining the check, and the cashier watched the keen face for a few moments.

"You seem greatly startled by the amount, Mr. Carter," he ventured presently. "Please tell me if there's anything out of the way. I had my doubts about it—owing solely to the size of the check; therefore I kept the man waiting until I had sent around to the hotel to make sure, but neither Mr. Stone nor his friend Mr. Crawford, who also has a large sum on deposit, was within reach."

"Did Follansbee present the check?"

"Oh, no. It was a young man who looked like a rather superior sort of servant, and who spoke English with a slight accent—German or Austrian, I think. The check was endorsed, as you see, and the man brought with him not only that note purporting to be signed by Mr. Stone, but also one from Doctor Follansbee on St.

Swithin's stationery. Here it is."

He handed Nick another sheet, bearing Follansbee's signature under an authorization to cash the check for his agent.

"That's undoubtedly genuine," the cashier went on. "I called up Doctor Follansbee at the hospital, and he assured me that everything was regular. There didn't seem to be anything to do but to take his word for it, owing to his position and reputation. It seemed very queer, though, and I couldn't understand why he didn't send the check to his own bank and let it take the usual course."

"You cashed it, then, in currency?"

"Yes, the man brought along a hand bag and carried away the money in it."

"Did you mark any of the bills?"

"Yes; many of those of large denomination. I felt compelled to take that precaution, although it seemed foolish. There were too many of them, though, to mark anywhere near all."

Carter leaned forward suddenly, and, holding Stone's note and the check together, placed them in front of the cashier.

"Do you notice any striking peculiarities about these two documents?" he asked.

The bank official scrutinized them carefully.

"I don't quite know what you mean," he said at length. "Oh, I think I see. All except the signature of the check seems to be written in another hand—more like Follansbee's than Stone's. Is that it?"

"That the most obvious," the detective answered. "It hints that Stone was foolish enough to sign a blank check or something of that sort. That isn't all, though. One would naturally assume that the check and Stone's note authorizing the payment had been written at the same time, yet I'd swear the ink on this check is older—perhaps several days older—than that on the note. What's more, I happen to know that, although this note is written on hotel paper, the ink used is not the shade of that furnished at the Windermere."

"By George!" muttered the cashier. "This is getting serious. You don't mean to tell me that Doctor Stephen Follansbee is a scamp?"

"These things speak for themselves, don't they?" Nick asked quietly. "And there are other straws which show the way the wind is blowing."

"What, for instance?"

CHAPTER XXXV.

THE DOCTOR GETS A SURPRISE.

The fires were now burning brightly in the great detective's eyes.

"I'm of the opinion that this note isn't more than a few hours old," he said, tapping the paper signed by Stone. "The ink is still fresh, and, besides, there's the date—the twenty-fifth."

"What of that?" demanded the cashier. "The check is also dated to-day."

"But it wasn't made out to-day."

"Still, I don't see what you're driving at. The check may have been dated ahead, and when the time approached for presenting it, Follansbee might have asked for the note to present along with it."

"Doubtless that's what happened, but what I'm getting at is this:

"This note purports to have been written at the Hotel Windermere on the twenty-fifth—to-day. I happen to know, however, that Stone hasn't been at the hotel since about three o'clock this morning, and I'm pretty well aware of the manner in which he was occupied while he was there. It isn't likely that he wrote this note between midnight and three o'clock, and even if he did do so, it isn't probable that he would have dated it to-day. Under such circumstances a man would jot down the date of the day before, nine times out of ten."

"Then you think that the note was written after he left the hotel?"

"I do, and I believe that the paper was thoughtfully given to him for the purpose, after having previously been removed from the hotel. That in itself is suspicious. It suggests a plot, and it, together with the character of the writing, hints that the note was written under pressure, or that Stone was not himself when he scribbled it. You can see the difference between the note, signature and all, and the signature on the check. The latter is big and bold and careless, but the note, although obviously written in the same hand, is tremulous and betrays agitation."

Expert as he was, Carter was a little astray there. He was not in a position to know that the agitation revealed had been due not to any threats of Follansbee's, but to the fact that Stone had been sane once more when he wrote it, and was suffering from the effects of his recent alarm and remorse.

As for his reasoning concerning the date on the note, it was sound enough in general, but the fact was the note had been written at Follansbee's, and that one of the doctor's servants, before retiring for the night, had torn off the sheet on the top of the pad calendar on the desk. That bearing the date of the twenty-fourth, had consequently gone into the waste basket, and the following date had been revealed in anticipation of the next day. Stone had glanced at this, and mechanically copied it.

"Then you think that this check and note were written under undue influence?" queried the cashier.

Nick nodded emphatically.

"There isn't the slightest doubt about it," he answered. "As a matter of fact, Stone has been suffering for months from some obscure mental trouble, and that is what took him to Doctor Follansbee."

"Is it possible!" whispered the bank official. "That's very unfortunate. We couldn't be expected to know that, though; and, after all, I hardly see what other course we could have followed."

"Oh, that's all right," Nick assured him. "The bank can't be blamed. It was an unusual proceeding, but you had ample justification for honoring the check, and you did what you could to get hold of Stone or his partner before doing so."

A relieved look spread over the cashier's face.

"I'm glad to hear you say that, Mr. Carter," he declared gravely. "Both the president and vice president are out of town, and this thing is up to me. As a matter of fact, it seems to me that Mr. Stone oughtn't to have been allowed to handle so much money if he's in the state you say he is. We're not alienists, and we would never have expected such a thing. Besides, the check would not have been honored had it not been made out to a man of such prominence who personally vouched for the proceeding, as he did over the telephone."

"I understand," Nick said consolingly. "Don't worry about your end of it. I think I can promise you that there won't be any comeback. It's up to me, though, to repair the damage, if I can. I had come to fear something of this sort in the last few hours, but Follansbee has stolen a march on me. I don't think his methods do any very great credit to his undoubted shrewdness, though, and the evidence you have to offer ought to be enough to make it hot for him."

He left a few minutes later, after promising to keep the bank informed of developments.

"Follansbee has made the haul of his life," Nick thought, as he paced along the busy street on his way back to the hotel; "and evidently Crawford wasn't his only victim."

When he reached the Windermere, his first act was to inquire if Stone had returned or if anything had been heard from him.

"Nothing doing," was the clerk's answer. "We're somewhat alarmed, Mr. Mortimer. We don't see how he could have left his room without the knowledge of the floor clerk."

Nick looked about and saw there was no one else within earshot. He leaned confidentially over the desk.

"I know how he left the building," he told the clerk; "and although I don't feel at liberty to tell you the whole story, I'll say this much: I'm Nicholas Carter, not Thomas Mortimer, and I have been keeping an eye on Stone and Crawford—for their good."

"You don't mean it!" cried the clerk, eying Nick's make-up inquiringly. "I hope they haven't done anything——"

"Nothing of that sort," Nick assured him quickly. "It's a long story, and the time hasn't come to tell it. Just keep it dark, therefore. I revealed my identity to your house detective last night, but I don't want it to be generally known that I've been here in disguise."

"Trust me, Mr. Carter; I understand. Is Mr. Crawford really ill, though?"

Nick gave a slow wink. "No, he isn't," he admitted. "I put that one over on you for reasons of my own, and I want you to pass the story on to any one who inquires after him. He won't be back for a few days, but you're to hold his room for him. I'll be responsible."

"And Mr. Stone?"

"I think I know where to find him, and I'm going to trace him without delay. Something may have happened to him, but nothing very serious, I'm sure. I'm going to give up my room now, since there doesn't seem to be anything else I can do here. By the way, I have reason to believe that the young man who phoned for me and called here later is one of my assistants. If he asks for me again after I leave, try to find out his identity without letting the cat out of the bag, and if he satisfies you, tell him I've gone home."

It was after two o'clock when Nick arrived at the house uptown, where he inquired first for Chick and then for Patsy Garvan. His housekeeper informed him that Chick was in Providence, and that Patsy had seemed very anxious to reach his fellow assistant or his chief that morning.

"You don't know why?"

"No, sir, I don't; but I think it is something important. He's been out every night lately, and goodness knows what time he's been coming in. He slept until half past eleven this morning, and that's why he missed Mr. Chick."

"Did he say where he was going?"

"No, sir."

It was plain that Patsy had stumbled over something important and was badly in need of advice, but it did not occur to the detective that it could have anything to do with Follansbee or Stone. He had given out no assignment of that sort. He found several matters which demanded his attention, and spent some time at his headquarters. He was impatient for the next move, but delayed a little in the hope that Patsy would put in an appearance. At length, however, having heard nothing from his young assistant, he determined on a bold step—nothing less than to seek out Doctor Follansbee and confront the cunning rogue with the evidence he had gathered.

"It's doubtful if I will be able to bring him to terms," he told himself, "for I doubt if he has a nerve in his body. It's worth trying, though. If he realizes that I've taken up the case, it will make him move more cautiously than he otherwise would. Besides, I must find out, if possible, what has happened to Stone. Poor Crawford will be on pins and needles until I can send him some definite word; and let's hope the news won't be too bad. Follansbee certainly means no good to Stone. He has annexed practically the whole of the fortune, and that implies some scheme to get rid of his victim. I'd be afraid that the worst had happened if I did not feel sure that Follansbee isn't the man to make use of any ordinary means of gaining his ends."

The detective hunted up Doctor Follansbee's private address in the telephone book and began hasty preparations for departure. He had already removed his disguise, and did not consider another. He meant to go openly in one of his cars and to see if he could scare the head of St. Swithin's into returning the money and dropping all of his schemes against the partners.

It was shortly after four o'clock when his machine stopped in front of the doctor's house and he strode up the steps. He was more than half prepared to find that Follansbee was out, although he had called up the hospital and learned that the doctor was not there. On the contrary, however, the servant informed him that her employer was at home.

Nick thought best not to give his name, and was ushered into the reception room as if he had been an ordinary patient without an appointment. But Follansbee happened to be at liberty, and in a few moments the servant invited him into the office adjoining the reception room.

It was a dark day, and the electric lights were on in the office. Nick stepped quietly into the room, and the light fell full upon his face. Follansbee did not look up at first, but when he became conscious that his visitor was standing just inside the door, he turned round to motion him to a seat. As he caught sight of the detective, he gave a visible start, and the hand on the desk closed convulsively.

His cool self-command had deserted him for the moment when he found himself face to face with the man who had once thwarted him and threatened to crush him if he ever broke his parole.

CHAPTER XXXVI.
SOME PLAIN TRUTHS.

Stephen Follansbee's loss of nerve was only momentary, however, and, after their looks had met, Nick quietly closed the door behind him, and, striding forward, dropped into a chair.

Follansbee looked at him with half-closed eyes and tapped on the desk with his long fingers. "This is an unexpected pleasure, Mr. Carter," he said, in his high, thin voice. "Of course I'm always glad to see such a distinguished visitor as yourself."

Nick's smile was grim. He rated his antagonist's recovered coolness and quiet irony at their true value. Physically, Follansbee was beneath contempt, but Nick was well aware that he represented an infinitely more dangerous type of criminal than any hulking, broad-shouldered ruffian who ever swaggered through the world.

"You did not come to see me on professional business, I take it?" Follansbee went on, a quiet smile lifting the corners of his mouth. "You don't look as if you needed medical attention."

"No, I'm quite well, thank you," was the calm response. "I have come to see you concerning a certain case I have taken up."

"Indeed?"

The doctor's voice was mildly curious, but there was a perceptible tightening of his fingers which told Nick that the man was holding himself in by sheer force of will.

"Yes," the detective continued; "recently I've had cause to play the part of a sort of bodyguard to a man who has just returned to this country from South America. His name is Winthrop Crawford."

Follansbee's performance was improving, in spite of the increasing strain under which he was laboring.

"That doesn't sound like a very important task for one of your abilities," remarked the physician. "What were your duties, may I ask?"

They were fencing with each other—fencing with the skill of masters—and Nick set himself to his task with keen zest.

"I undertook the part of bodyguard to Crawford," he explained, "in order that he might be safe from the murderous attacks of his former friend and partner,

James Stone."

"Oh!" Follansbee played with the pen on his desk. "All this may be very interesting to you," he said presently, "but I can't imagine what it has to do with me. If you can enlighten me as to that, perhaps I shall prove a better listener."

Nick leaned forward quickly, and his clean-cut face was grave and hard. "On second thoughts, I suggest that we throw aside our masks, and go at it face to face," he said. "I'm telling you this for the very good reason that to my personal knowledge you had a hand in the last fiendish attack which Stone made on Crawford."

Follansbee raised his vulturelike face and shot a keen glance at the detective.

"I suppose you're quite sane," he said slowly, "although your statements sound curiously wild. You deliberately accuse me of having connived with some man of whose identity I am ignorant, to murder some one?"

"I do!" Nick rapped out. "And the reason I accuse you of it is that I saw you—and heard you—conspiring with Stone last night in his room at the Hotel Windermere."

"Good Lord!"

Stephen Follansbee had betrayed himself. His icy self-command had cracked for a moment, and through the fissure Nick saw a flicker of fear in the beady eyes.

"Ah! I found a joint in your armor that time, didn't I? Shall I tell you what you did at the hotel?"

But the head of St. Swithin's held himself once more with a tight rein. He leaned back in his chair and folded his arms.

"I'm afraid you misinterpreted my exclamation," he said. "It was called out not by guilt, but by astonishment and concern. My confidence in your sanity has received a big jolt, Carter. I've been treated to many such flights of the imagination, but I never expected to find you indulging in them. Professionally, though, your condition appeals to me, and I'm tempted to humor you; therefore, go on by all means, and tell me what I did at the—what hotel did you say it was?"

"Cut it out, Follansbee," the detective advised, ignoring the question. "You've given yourself away, and it's a waste of cleverness to try to cover up the break now. I'll accept your invitation, though, and tell you what you did. In the first place, you were unconventional enough to choose the fire escape as a means of access to Stone's room."

He did not look into Follansbee's eyes, but fastened his gaze on the man's right temple. The eyes would have told him nothing, but there was a blue, distended vein in that temple, and its throbbing was significant.

"You and your patient—your tool—used a painter's ladder to reach the fire escape," the detective went on, "and when you had climbed to Stone's room, on the second floor, you neglected to remove a little wedge of wood on the sill which prevented the sash from closing."

He leaned farther forward, and his voice was the voice of a judge. "Thanks to that little oversight, Follansbee," he continued, "I was able to hear all that you said. I heard from your own lips about the hypodermic syringe, and the character of its contents, as well as about the drug which you gave to Stone to— —

"Keep your hands up!"

CHAPTER XXXVII.

FOLLANSBEE REACHES THE LIMIT.

The sudden command had been fully justified.

One of Follansbee's long, lean hands crept to his side—the side away from the detective—and had been extended toward an open drawer in the desk.

Nick did not wait to see whether his order met with obedience or not. The words were still on his lips when he leaped to his feet and flung himself across the intervening space, grasping the thin, steel-like wrists of the physician.

The grip brought Follansbee to his feet, and for a moment the two faced each other, their eyes flashing. Perhaps the powerful grip of the detective's fingers had warned Follansbee of the uselessness of a struggle, but the unmasked, flaming rage in his face revealed the depth of his hatred.

A quiet smile flitted over the detective's features. He quietly brought Follansbee's two wrists together, clasped them both with the fingers of one hand, and then leaning down, pulled out the open drawer a little farther.

As he had anticipated, he found a revolver in it. This he confiscated and dropped it into his pocket.

"I'll take charge of this," he announced. "All the same, though, I don't trust you, and I must ask you to keep your hands on the desk hereafter. If you don't, you may get hurt."

With that he released Follansbee and stepped back. The head of St. Swithin's glared at him for a few brief moments, then subsided into his chair again, and, with a sullen, venomous look, leaned both arms on the desk.

"I suppose there's no use in playing the part any longer," he confessed.

Nick pricked up his ears at this and wondered if it were possible that Follansbee was about to make a clean breast of it. The latter's next words, however, proved that the hope was groundless.

"I was at the Windermere last night," Follansbee declared coolly, "but not for the reason you think. James Stone is my patient, and that's why I consented to go through with that rather questionable farce. I can hardly blame you for misinterpreting it, but the fact remains——"

"Drop it!" Nick broke in. "I can guess what you're going to say. You're going to tell me that you were merely 'humoring' Stone in an attempt to draw him out and get to the root of his disease. I suppose you think I'm green enough to believe that there was nothing harmful in that syringe."

"Nothing worse than glycerine," the physician assured him.

Nick's laugh was harsh.

"You're a fool, Follansbee," he declared. "You think you're so clever that you can't make yourself believe the other fellow has any brains at all."

"Do you think a man of my standing would deliberately lie?"

The detective might have said that he knew Follansbee was lying, but he did not choose to do so for the very good reason that he did not wish the doctor to learn just then what he had done.

"Standing hasn't anything to do with it," he answered. "It's your personality I don't trust, Follansbee."

The physician's lips curled cynically. "That's my misfortune—or yours," he said. "You played the spy last night and heard some things which could easily be twisted. Your interpretation is wide of the mark, however, and even if it were not, more than one witness would be required to give any weight to the evidence. You couldn't prove anything against me if you tried, and I'm sure you're too sensible to try. I have no personal knowledge of the matter, but I'll wager that your friend is perfectly well and sound to-day. If he isn't, it's no fault of mine."

"What's the good of this fencing?" demanded the detective. "Of course Crawford is all right—so far as you know. That's understood, and was provided for in your instructions to your tool. The stuff isn't supposed to act at once, and that's why you chose it. We'll come back to that later on. What I want to make clear now is that I know exactly what you've done and that I also know you have already realized on your crime."

Doctor Follansbee stiffened a little. "Realized on my crime?" he cried. "What do you mean by that?"

"Precisely what I say," Nick answered coolly. "I happened to make a call early this afternoon at a certain bank not far from the Hotel Windermere, and I had a very interesting interview with its cashier. He showed me three decidedly noteworthy documents—a note from you, one from James Stone, and last, but not least, a check signed by Stone, but otherwise filled in by you. It called for a huge amount, and had been cashed just before the bank closed."

Follansbee's control was amazing.

"Well, what of it?" he snarled. "Everything was regular, wasn't it? Surely you haven't any doubt of the genuineness of Stone's note? As for the check, it was for a large sum, I'll admit, but every one knows that I exact large fees, and if a patient chooses to consider my services worth that much, it's none of your business."

"Isn't it? I'm afraid you're mistaken there, Follansbee. Picture to yourself what it will mean when this thing comes out; when the world learns that you have obtained nearly half a million dollars by swindling a patient who trusted himself to you, and whose unsound mind made him an easy victim. How long do you think you will hold your position at the head of St. Swithin's? And how many of your rich patients will employ you again when it is known that you used disappearing ink to gain your unscrupulous ends? Ah, I see that gets under your skin!"

The detective paused for a moment and watched the discomfited rascal through narrowed lids.

"I thought at first that Stone had merely signed the check in blank," he continued, "which would have implied a greater mental lack on his part and a lesser degree of criminality on yours; but now I know better. I took that check home with me, Follansbee, and examined it under a microscope. Thanks to that, I discovered that there had been other writing on it—doubtless in Stone's hand. Your trick ink had quite disappeared, but the point of the pen had slightly scratched the surface of the paper; and, moreover, the application of a chemical on one or two spots revealed traces of the ink originally used. As soon as the bank gives me permission to do so, I shall apply that chemical—you can doubtless guess what it is—to the whole check, and thereby bring out the original writing once more. And when I do so, I'm sure I shall find that, as Stone made it out, the check originally called for a much smaller sum. Doubtless you found some excuse to change inks when it came to the signature, with the result that it alone was written with ordinary ink. What do you say to that?"

Apparently Follansbee had nothing to say. His hands were clenched on his desk and he was biting his under lip and glaring fearfully at the detective. Nick returned look for look and allowed his glance to play over the surface of the desk. As it did so, it fell upon a letter which Follansbee had been writing before his visitor's entrance. The doctor's name and address were engraved in the upper left-hand corner, and the ink in which the beginning of the letter was written was of the same shade as that used on the three documents which the detective had obtained at the bank.

"That reminds me," said Nick, looking from the unfinished letter to the open ink bottle.

He paused, and then with a swift movement thrust his hand out, picked up the bottle, corked it, and started to drop it into his pocket.

"This will be one more link in the chain—your chain," he announced.

Snarling like a wild beast, and with an agility for which Nick had not given him credit, Follansbee shot out of his chair and hurled himself upon the detective.

In the brief tussle which followed, the tables were turned, despite the detective's greater bulk and strength.

CHAPTER XXXVIII.

NICK IS BALKED.

One of the little physician's hands shot out and caught at the ink bottle which the detective was about to pocket, and as they reeled across the room together, the rascal lowered his head unexpectedly and set his sharp teeth into Nick Carter's hand.

It was the trick of an animal rather than of a human being, and it took the detective completely by surprise.

Involuntarily Nick released his hold on the bottle, and it fell to the floor. The fall did not break it, however, and Follansbee was obliged to kick it into the fireplace, where it struck against one of the massive andirons and was shattered, its contents mixing with the ashes.

With a swift movement Nick released himself from his clinging antagonist, and sent him spinning after the broken bottle. The doctor recovered his balance, gasping for breath, and the two faced each other silently for a few moments.

"Well," Follansbee said presently, panting, "you didn't connect with that bit of evidence after all, did you?"

The detective shrugged his shoulders.

"True," he admitted. "I knew I was dealing with a cur, but I forgot that you weren't muzzled. You needn't pride yourself on your victory, however; the ink would have been a little further evidence against you, but I can very easily get along without it. But I didn't come here to bandy words with you, or to fight with mad dogs. I came to find out where your latest victim is—Stone, I mean; and I'd advise you not to put any more obstacles in my way."

"What do I know about Stone?"

"That's what I want you to tell me. I heard you arrange to wait for him outside the bank, and I saw you leave the hotel for that performance. He hasn't been back since, and the hotel people are beginning to worry about it. It is up to you to do a little explaining, if you don't want to be accused of another crime."

"I know nothing about it," the rascal insisted. "Stone came back here, it's true. I brought him in my car, and he was here for some little time. It must have been something after three o'clock when he left, intending to walk back to the hotel. That's the last I saw of him."

He spoke with the utmost assurance, and unfortunately Nick was not able to contradict him. The detective realized with a sinking of the heart that, in spite of Follansbee's telltale flareups and partial or implied confessions, the man intended to fight doggedly every step of the way.

For a moment he was at a loss to know how to proceed, and the Buzzard, seeing his hesitation, took advantage of that fact.

"That's all I have to tell you," Follansbee went on triumphantly. "Make as much—or as little—of it as you can. Let me remind you of something else, too. Any charge you may try to bring against me will involve Stone and give a lot of undesirable publicity to his mental condition. It will involve you, too, for if he's as dangerous as you claim he is, the newspapers and the public will ask why you allowed him to go about of his own free will, to live unmolested at a hotel, and all the rest of it. More than that, the revelations that will inevitably follow will make your friend Crawford very sore. He has stuck to Stone, I understand, through thick and thin. I don't pretend to say what his motives have been, but I know enough to be sure that he won't welcome the limelight when it's thrown upon them."

Nick was amazed at the man's cleverness in making use of such an argument. He had felt himself hampered at every turn by the peculiar circumstances which surrounded the case, and especially by Crawford's insistance that no punishment be visited upon his old partner. It had seemed to the detective, however, when he discovered the way in which Follansbee had juggled with the check, that he had the scoundrel where he wanted him, but now he was beginning to doubt even that. At any rate, he did not feel justified in having Follansbee arrested at once. He needed to know what had become of Stone before doing that, and it was desirable to have another conference with Crawford in order to see how far the latter was willing for him to go.

All of which meant that he was unprepared in many ways for the situation which had developed. It went decidedly against the grain, after having carried things so far, to be obliged to indulge only in empty words, and finally to walk out of Follansbee's house empty-handed. Yet that seemed to be what he was destined to do. Had he known what Patsy Garvan knew, he could have turned the tables very neatly, and might have brought Follansbee to time, but he did not have an inkling that his assistant's eagerness to see him had had any bearing on the case in hand.

"You refuse, then, to tell me where James Stone is?" he asked, harking back to his errand.

"I have told you all I know," the head of St. Swithin's declared sullenly. "I'm not running an insane asylum."

"And you're going to keep his fortune? You don't think it wise to make restitution, and thereby lighten your punishment?"

"I shall certainly not part with the money," was the answer. "I have earned it, or will earn it before I get through. If I'm let alone, James Stone will not be crazy when I have finished with him. As for any little irregularities there may have been about the transaction, that's a matter for Stone and Crawford to decide. It isn't any of your business or the public's, and if you're wise you won't try to take any steps against me."

He was still standing before the fireplace, and perceptibly trembling with rage. He clenched his hands now and bared his teeth.

"Have a care, Nicholas Carter," he went on shrilly. "I'm not the sort of man to allow another to cross my path with impunity. It would be far better for you to retire from this case right now, and leave matters as they stand. If you become a menace to me, I swear I'll sweep you out of my way." Here he passed his long, lean hand around, as though brushing away some object. "Let me tell you," he added, "that I'm a dangerous man to have for an enemy."

"Your threats haven't any weight with me, Follansbee," the detective answered quietly. "I've devoted my life to handling such blackguards as you. You're clever, but you're not clever enough; no scamp is. The evil he does trips him up sooner or later. I tell you here and now that you will not enjoy one penny of that money, no matter what happens. You may spend some of it, but you'll be looking for a thunderbolt all the time."

As he spoke, he half turned and approached the door. He took good care, however, to keep one eye on the physician, for he knew that at that moment Follansbee was ready for anything.

"I've given you your chance," the detective said, as he laid his hand on the knob, "and you haven't seen fit to take it. I can find Stone without aid, and when I do, you'll discover that you've made a bad bargain. Good afternoon."

The door closed behind the lithe figure, and Follansbee just for a moment allowed his stiff attitude to relax. It seemed as though the lean body shrank, that his clothes suddenly became too large for him. There was a curious mummylike expression about his sharp features as he leaned against the mantel.

"How much does he know?" he muttered to himself. "By heavens, it was well that I got rid of Stone when I did. I defy him to find out where he is now."

A sudden gust of anger swept over him, and he reeled toward the door, shaking his fists. "I defy you! I defy you!" he shrieked, in his thin voice. "Look out for yourself, Nick Carter! Men have died for less than you have done."

There was an unholy meaning in his voice, and the face looked fiendish in its menace. At that moment Stephen Follansbee looked what he was—an insatiable bird of prey. "Only let me get you into my power," he continued, "and nothing in the world will save you!"

Nick Carter had made another enemy; one whose scientific resources and unusual shrewdness might have daunted almost any one, when coupled, as they were, with the maddening thirst for revenge which shook him at that moment.

CHAPTER XXXIX.

PATSY TRACES THE AMBULANCE.

There is always a certain element of luck in one's experiences, and chance ordained it that Patsy Garvan should arrive in front of St. Swithin's Hospital at just the right moment. His anxiety had sent him in that direction after his repeated failures to reach his chief, but he had no very definite idea in view.

He had driven the little runabout to Amsterdam Avenue partly to kill time during his chief's absence from the hotel. Having left the car around the corner, he had approached the hospital on foot. When he came near the big entrance, he noticed an ambulance—evidently a private one, for there was no lettering on it—drawn up at the curb with a circle of the curious loitering about it. Evidently some patient was to be taken away in the ambulance; perhaps a convalescent. Patsy mingled with the crowd, but before he had time to make any inquiries, a couple of hospital attendants appeared, half carrying, half supporting a tall man.

One glance at the face was sufficient for Patsy. Despite the intense pallor which lay under the tan, he recognized it at once as being that of James Stone, whom he had previously taken pains to identify. The miner was fully dressed, but his eyes were sunken, and every line of his naturally powerful frame bespoke weakness and listlessness. The two attendants, although they were supporting Stone, were allowing him to make use of his lower limbs, and the mine owner was able to walk unsteadily toward the ambulance.

Nick's assistant looked about and into the wide hallway, but could see no signs of Doctor Follansbee. A dapper-looking interne in a white uniform was superintending the removal. When Stone had been placed in the vehicle, a stout, matronly looking nurse in uniform came out of the hospital and entered the waiting ambulance. Immediately the vehicle, a motor one, started quietly and shot ahead down the street.

Patsy bitterly regretted that he had left his runabout. If he had brought it to the front of the hospital he could have followed the ambulance, but as it was there was no hope of that. The ambulance was already a block away, and going at a high rate of speed, and there was no other available vehicle within reach.

"Confound it," thought the young detective. "Why didn't it have a sign on it? If it had I would have known where to look for Stone."

As a matter of fact, he did know where to look, although indirectly. He had to have something to worry about, however, for this succession of anticipated developments was getting on his nerves, and he felt very much aggrieved because he had been unable to share the knowledge of them with any one else. He had taken the precaution of fixing the license number of the ambulance in his memory before it had been whisked away, and he knew that all he had to do—unless the number was a false one—was to get into communication with the license bureau.

He chose to follow that line rather than to question the young interne, since the latter course might have aroused suspicion, and his questions might be reported to Follansbee. It involved some delay, but that could hardly be avoided, and the sight of Stone, though weak and ill, had reassured Patsy somewhat. At any rate, he knew now that the man was not dead, and there seemed to be no reason to believe that a few hours' further delay, if it came to that, would have very serious consequences.

Apparently Doctor Follansbee was playing an unusual game, and one that could not be brought to a conclusion at once. Patsy had no doubt that the head of St. Swithin's had planned this move from the beginning. Stone had probably been taken to the big hospital the night before merely as a temporary expedient, and to lend an appearance of regularity to the proceedings. Now he was being removed to some place where Follansbee would find himself less hampered in his dealings with him.

The crowd had quickly melted away, and the young interne and the hospital attendants had reëntered the big building while Patsy stood staring after the vanishing ambulance. Now he strode away and returned to his own car. Entering it, he drove a few blocks and stopped in front of a telephone pay station. After a little delay he obtained the number of the license bureau, and asked for the name of the institution owning the designated machine.

It was two or three minutes before he received a reply, but when it came, it told him all that he needed to know for the time being.

"Nineteen-nineteen license, number five hundred and fifty thousand, three hundred and thirteen, New York, is issued in the name of Miss Worth's Private Hospital for Convalescents, fifteen thousand Flatbush Avenue, Brooklyn," he was told.

Patsy thanked his informant, to whom he had been obliged to give his name in order to obtain the desired information. When he had reached the street again he paused before entering the runabout.

"Now, it's up to me to make another stab at an interview with the chief," he thought. "If I don't catch him this time, I'll begin to think I'm the victim of a jinx."

He entered the little car and headed back to the Hotel Windermere. There he received another slap. Nick had been in and left, but the clerk questioned Patsy as the detective had suggested, and satisfied himself of his identity. The young assistant learned in this way that his chief had revealed himself to the clerk, and had left word that he was going back home.

He swallowed his disappointment as best he could, and felt sure that the trail must be nearing its end. He had no doubt that he would find his chief when he reached the house.

But Fate took the next trick away from him also.

CHAPTER XL.

THE PRIVATE HOSPITAL.

In his eagerness to reach the detective's headquarters, Patsy drove the runabout rather recklessly at a time when the streets were full of traffic. As a result, his machine was struck by a street car, and he was thrown out against the curbstone. He was rendered unconscious and removed to the hospital, where, owing to the fact that he was in disguise, his identity was not discovered.

When he came to, he felt decidedly groggy at first, but insisted on dressing and leaving the hospital. After he had given his name, he was allowed to go under protest, and a taxi was sent for.

The hired machine took him home in record time, but when he arrived there, the chief had once more flown. To be sure, he had left word that he was going to Doctor Follansbee's, but that only added to Patsy's troubles.

On the one side, the young assistant felt it to be his duty to follow his chief immediately and reveal what he had learned, in the hope that his information would clinch the case against the doctor, and leave the latter no loophole or escape. On the other hand, however, he found himself hesitating and undecided. He did not know why his chief had gone to the physician's house, and was afraid to spoil Nick's plans in some way. The detective might be working under cover in such a way that Patsy's coming would ruin everything. Anyway, even at best, it would be decidedly awkward for him to break in on an interview without previously preparing his superior for his revelations, or finding out if they would be welcome at that time.

If he only could have caught his chief before the latter had left, all would have been well, but as it was, Nick might already have left Follansbee's, and Patsy's inquiries for him might alarm the physician and lead to further complications.

"This is certainly my unlucky day," Nick's assistant complained inwardly. "What the dickens am I to do now? I could sit here and twiddle my thumbs, of course, while waiting for the chief to show up, but every time I get busy, I seem to learn something more of importance—something that the chief isn't wise to. I think, therefore, I'll have another try at the same game."

He was already feeling much better, and a bath and a change of clothing left few traces of his recent accident. Before leaving the house, he scribbled a brief note to his chief and left it with the housekeeper. It read:

"DEAR CHIEF: I have been having a mischief of a time trying to locate you. I am bursting with information about Stone and Follansbee, but have decided not to run the risk of spoiling your play by following you to the latter's house. Stone has been removed from St. Swithin's Hospital to Miss Worth's private hospital for convalescents, on Flatbush Avenue. I saw him when he was put into the ambulance. He looked considerably the worse for wear, but was walking—with assistance. I'm going over to Brooklyn now to murder a little more time while waiting for you. For the love of Mike stay put this time until I can get back!

P.G."

Young Garvan had already put one car out of commission that day, and did not know where it was, although he assumed that it was in the hands of the police—if there was anything left of it. That was only an incident in the day's work, however, and he promptly sent for another of the detective's machines.

In it he hurried downtown across the Manhattan Bridge, and sped up Flatbush Avenue. He had learned so much that he hoped to pick up some more information. Nick might know something about Miss Worth's hospital, but he did not, and he wished to supply that deficiency if he could. This time he had brought the detective's chauffeur along with him, and he remained with the car when Patsy left it a block or two from his destination.

It was an easy matter to find the private hospital, although the small brass plate affixed to one of the big gate posts was the only outward evidence that the building was more than a private residence. It was a large, old-fashioned house, with broad verandas, standing some distance back from the street, in the midst of extensive grounds. A driveway led up to the spacious entrance, and in this drive, just in front of the door, stood a handsome motor vehicle. Patsy's experiences of the night before had familiarized with just such a car, and his nerves tingled as he caught sight of it.

"Follansbee's own machine, as I'm a living sinner," he thought, with a start. "The last time I saw that was when the doctor brought Stone home with him in the small hours of the morning. This is interesting, to say the least. That rascal hasn't lost much time before paying a visit to his 'patient' in the latter's surroundings."

The sight of the car changed his plans. He had intended to pay a visit to the private hospital at once, but now he decided to delay until Follansbee had left.

He strolled up and down the block for perhaps ten minutes, and at the end of that time his patience was rewarded. He saw the diminutive, sinister form of Stephen Follansbee emerge from Miss Worth's and vanish into the vehicle, which promptly wheeled and made its way back to the city. When it had gone, Patsy sauntered slowly along the pavement, and paused for a moment in front of the gate. He was anxious to find out what kind of a place it was; and at last, putting on a bold front, he entered the grounds, strode up the walk, and rang the bell.

A neat-looking maid opened the door to him, and he was led into a quiet waiting room.

Patsy always had a story ready to fit the occasion, and it was generally the most plausible sort; consequently, he was quite prepared for the advent of Miss Worth herself, who proved to be a kindly-faced woman of middle age, gray-haired and stately.

He informed the lady that a friend of his was convalescent after a fever, but that certain unavoidable noises in the neighborhood made him nervous, and it seemed best to remove him to a more quiet place. Patsy, it appeared, had taken upon himself to hunt up such a place, and, having been told of Miss Worth's, had called to inquire as to the charges.

His well-cut suit and his ingratiating manner had their effect. After giving him the information he asked for, Miss Worth volunteered to show him over the building, and Patsy spent fifteen minutes in going through the wards. It was soon obvious to him that the private hospital was a perfectly respectable place, and the well-bred face of Miss Worth herself justified the opinion that she could have nothing in common with the scoundrelly side of Stephen Follansbee.

Presently the lady paused in front of a door and opened it.

"There's a new guest here," she said: "a poor fellow who is recovering from the effects of the drug habit."

Patsy glanced into the room and noted that there were two beds in it. The one on the right was unoccupied, but in the left one lay the figure of James Stone. The ex-miner's eyes were closed, and his hands stretched out on top of the coverlet were painfully clenched.

"Our distinguished consultant, Doctor Stephen Follansbee, of St. Swithin's Hospital, has made a special study of that type of case," Miss Worth went on, as she closed the door. "The patient will soon recover, and meanwhile your friend could have that other bed. It happens to be the only one available just now."

"What luck!" thought Patsy. "It's a good thing I took it into my head to come over here. I hope the chief will appreciate all I've done. Hanged if I can see how he thought he could handle this case alone."

Assuring Miss Worth that he would let her know as soon as possible of his friend's decision, he left the building. He was on tenterhooks now to pour out the whole story to his chief, and as soon as he was out of sight from the hospital windows, he hurried to the waiting car.

"Start something!" he urged the chauffeur. "Open her up and let's see you burn up a little asphalt."

CHAPTER XLI.

NICK HAS A PLAN.

Darkness had descended when Patsy sprang up the steps of Nick Carter's house. He eagerly inquired for his chief, and learned, to his delight, that he had returned and was in his study. The young assistant fairly sprinted up the stairs, and burst into the room.

"Well!" he ejaculated. "I began to think I'd never see you again."

"I usually bob up sooner or later," was the answer. "What's all this you've been up to? How did you break into this game, I'd like to know?"

"That's just what I did—I broke in," was the answer. "Chick put me up to it. He was itching to have a hand in the affair, and had a hunch that somebody ought to keep an eye on Follansbee. He couldn't do it himself, because you had left him in charge of affairs, and so I've been losing my beauty sleep—and most of the rest—for several nights. Nothing happened until last night, but since then things have been coming so thick and fast that they've taken my breath away."

Nick tried to look stern. "You don't seem to realize that this is a breach of discipline," he commented.

"Now, chief, don't be nasty about it," Patsy pleaded. "Let me get this out of my system. My private information is that you couldn't have done without me, and when I get through, I think you'll agree that I haven't wasted my time."

The detective smiled slightly. "Go ahead and let's hear it," he said. "You usually get your way in the end."

After some little beating around, young Garvan launched into an account of his adventures from the time Follansbee and Stone had arrived at the former's house, until the last glimpse of the miner had been obtained at the private hospital. The look of interest and satisfaction which came into the great detective's face assured Patsy that he was pardoned.

As a matter of fact, the assistant's report, coupled with what Nick had learned for himself, brought the whole case to a focus, and made plain much that had seemed obscure.

"By George, my boy," the chief commented at the end of the recital, "you certainly have turned a trick or two, and I wish I had known something about it before I bearded Follansbee in his den. If I had, it would have put a very different face on that interview. I was all up in the air about Stone, but now everything is clear enough and— —"

"Then you're better off than I am, chief," his assistant interrupted, "for I can't make head or tail of it. I thought it was Crawford that that scoundrel Follansbee was plotting against, but it can hardly be doubted that Stone is his victim—or one of them, at least."

"I will give you a little information to complete the exchange," was the answer.

In a few brief sentences the detective gave Patsy his side of the story, and the young man's eyes fairly flashed as he heard the grim details of the attempt on Winthrop Crawford's life.

"What a fiend that man Follansbee is!" Patsy exclaimed at the end. "Thank Heaven you were on hand to ditch his scheme. But what do you make of it now? What do you think Follansbee is up to in connection with Stone?"

"I can't say offhand," was the reply. "Not a little remains to be seen. I had thought that Stone might be in hiding somewhere, suffering from a guilty conscience; but, on the whole, I was inclined to believe that Follansbee had drawn him into the net. Your revelations leave no doubt of that, and seem to indicate that we have time enough to save Stone. He needs saving, though, that's certain. So far as I can tell, Follansbee still believes that Stone injected the serum given him for that purpose, and that Crawford is doomed. I was skating on thin ice this afternoon in my interview with the fellow. I didn't want him to know that I had thwarted him, but I looked for him to guess it.

"He ought to have realized at once that, after I had heard his conversation with Stone, I wouldn't have stood by and allowed the latter to make the injection, knowing as I do what it would have meant. Evidently, however, he thinks I didn't interfere. He has Stone's word for it, of course, that the hypodermic was used as directed."

"That must be it," agreed Patsy. "You were speaking of Follansbee's attitude toward Stone, though, and the urgent need of interference."

"Exactly. I was going to say that since the rascal apparently thinks the injection was made as planned, he's convinced he has a strangle hold on Stone. He's cleaned out the latter's fortune, and can keep him cowed by drugs and threats. That may be what he plans to do for the present, in anticipation of Crawford's death. Stone, as I told you, is named as the chief beneficiary in Crawford's will, and if Follansbee could keep Stone alive and in his power until Crawford passes out, there would be another half a million or so to angle for."

"Great Scott! You mean that Follansbee intends to wait until Stone becomes Crawford's legal heir, and then plans to swindle Stone out of Crawford's fortune, as well as the poor devil's own?"

"It wouldn't surprise me in the least; and when that was accomplished, there wouldn't be any doubt about the next step. Stone would surely die in turn, but in such a way that no one could prove anything suspicious about his death."

Patsy whistled softly. "It's a large order," he remarked; "but that check for four hundred and fifty thousand shows that Follansbee is capable of thinking in big numbers. You're probably right, therefore; but there's something about it that beats me."

"What's that?"

"I can't understand how Follansbee would dare to go so far. It might be impossible to prove anything, but the very fact that Stone had been a patient of his, and that he had realized a huge sum through the association would look pretty bad on the face of it; wouldn't it? It might not bring conviction, but it could hardly fail to be the means of severing Follansbee from his job as the head of St. Swithin's, and of cutting off his practice. More than that, though, he's aware that you know what he's up to, and that you're right after him. I can't conceive of his going on with it under the circumstances."

Nick smiled grimly. "Follansbee is an extraordinary man," he answered. "As you say, he already knows that I have a lot of dangerous evidence against him. That very thing, though, may drive him on to fresh crimes, on the theory that he might as well be killed for a sheep as a lamb. If he thinks Crawford is doomed — as he evidently does — another life is of no consequence. I suspect that he really counts on getting rid of me. He implied as much this afternoon. If he tries that, though, he'll have his hands full, shrewd as he is."

Nick got up suddenly. "Enough of this," he said. "We might keep on theorizing all night, but I prefer action."

"What are you going to do?"

"I'm going to try to sound Stone, if possible, and that's where you'll come in." He nodded to his assistant. "I'm going to make use of that nice little introduction you prepared for me at Miss Worth's," he added significantly.

Patsy was on his feet at once. "You don't mean to say — —" he began.

Nick smiled. "Precisely," he replied. "I'm going to occupy that bed next to Stone. I'll be your convalescent friend."

CHAPTER XLII.

THE DETECTIVE ACQUIRES A WIFE.

"Now, then, my boy," the detective went on, pointing to the telephone on his desk, "you'll oblige me by calling up Miss Worth and telling her that your friend has agreed to place himself in her hands. Say that he'll arrive there about half past nine to-night."

Patsy eyed his chief doubtfully. "It's a risky business," he warned him. "You'll have to stay there for some time to keep up the bluff, and Follansbee will probably visit Stone to-morrow. If the scoundrel should recognize you— —"

"I'll take that risk," Nick put in; "but I don't think he will. If I can't make use of a disguise that will deceive him, I ought to go out of the business. It's settled, any-way. I want you to accompany me to Miss Worth's and see me safely deposited."

"How long do you expect to stay there?"

"I haven't the slightest idea. That will depend on circumstances. Perhaps I can get away after a day, but it may be a week, for all I know." And he left the room.

Patsy nodded after the lithe, upright figure. "I'll give you twenty-four hours, chief," he said to himself; "and if you're not out of that place by that time, I'll be hanged if I don't come and get you."

He turned to the desk, and, after consulting the telephone book, found the number of Miss Worth's private hospital.

"Number two bed in Ward E will be reserved for your friend, Mr. Bainbridge," Miss Worth informed him over the wire. Gerald Bainbridge was the name Patsy had given to Nick on the spur of the moment.

About nine o'clock that evening young Garvan, who was fidgeting about in the study, heard the door open softly. Some one entered the room. He knew that it was his chief, but he was forced to think that the disguise was one of the most suc-cessful Nick had ever attempted. He had dressed himself in a suit that was a size or two too large for him. The garments hung loosely on him, he stooped slightly, and it seemed as though his shoulders were much thinner and narrower than was actually the case. His cheeks looked hollow and his eyes had dark rings around them that seemed to indicate a weakened frame and long hours on a sick bed. A straggling beard, badly in need of trimming, covered his cheeks and chin. It was by no means an ordinary false one, but one of Nick's own invention—of the kind used by him when the occasion called for extraordinary care against detection.

He knew that he would be in charge of a nurse, and that a commonplace disguise would not stand the close inspection he would be obliged to undergo. It would have taken a Nick Carter himself, however, to discover that that beard was artificial. It had been put on with a great deal of care, and the thin substance into which the hairs were embedded so closely resembled the human skin in hue and texture that it was almost impossible to tell where one began and the other left off. Ordinary washing would not effect it in the least, and yet it could be removed in fifteen minutes' time—if one knew how. It was the same with the wig.

He was leaning heavily on a stout walking stick, and caught the look of admiration in Patsy's eyes.

"Well, will I do?" he asked.

His assistant drew a deep breath. "You're the real thing," was the enthusiastic comment. "I never saw you turn out anything better than that."

A moment later Ida Jones, Nick's beautiful woman assistant, entered the room. She, too, was to play a part in the sketch that had been so hastily staged. Nick waved one trembling hand toward her.

"For an old friend, my boy, you don't seem to be on your job. Is it possible you don't recognize 'Mrs. Bainbridge?'"

Patsy looked bewildered for a moment, and then broke into a grin. "Mrs. Bainbridge, eh?" he queried. "So you've taken a wife for the occasion, have you? Is she going with us?"

"Of course. She's devoted to her husband, and it wouldn't do, you know, for you to take me there alone. We'll have to have a woman along to fuss over me and make the thing seem real."

The young assistant's grin broadened. "Well, I must say I admire your taste," he remarked, with a wink. "I could have told you long ago that Ida is just the girl for you."

Miss Jones laughed. "None of that, Patsy," she said laughingly. "If the chief ever comes to think of me as a girl, he'll fire me as sure as fate."

Nick looked at her admiringly. "I'm not quite as bad as that, Ida," he said. "Give me credit, please, for knowing that you're a girl, and a remarkably attractive one. But you're a corking good detective, also, and I'm afraid that interests me more. No more nonsense now, you two. It's time to go."

A couple of travel-worn suit cases had been provided and packed. Catching these up, Patsy went off down the stairs, followed by Nick and the girl.

About half an hour later their machine—a hired taxi—halted at Miss Worth's steps. Patsy and the girl jumped out and solicitously helped their companion to alight, while the chauffeur rang the bell. Miss Worth herself followed the servant to the door, and all concerned played their parts to perfection. Patsy was a rather officious, but tender-hearted friend. Ida Jones made a beautiful and devoted wife, while Nick assumed a querulous voice and a crotchety manner which went well with his apparent weakness.

"I don't want any nurses fussing about me, except when it is absolutely necessary," he declared. "I've had quite enough of nurses. I want just a quiet, peaceful time, you understand?"

Miss Worth assured him that he would have no cause to complain of overattention, and gave Mrs. Bainbridge a reassuring look behind his back.

Patsy was having all he could do to keep a straight face, and, indeed, when the others had left the reception room, he felt obliged to relax and indulge in a hearty, though silent, laugh. In a moment he became serious enough, however, when he remembered Follansbee's threats and the defenseless position in which his chief was placing himself.

Ida Jones had, of course, accompanied her "husband" to the room which he was to occupy. She had declared that she must see it, in order to be sure that he would be comfortable. Five minutes later, however, she returned to the waiting room, still escorted by Miss Worth, and, after leaving many parting injunctions, she accompanied Patsy out of the house.

"When the taxi starts, you must applaud, Patsy," she whispered, as they crossed the veranda. "I flatter myself that I did that fairly well."

"You certainly did," he answered. "You could give points to most wives—except mine."

He was thinking of something else though—of Stephen Follansbee's diabolical cleverness.

"Twenty-four hours is the most I'll allow the chief," he said, repeating his resolve. "If he isn't out by that time—unless I know everything is all right—I'm going to stick a finger into the pie once more."

CHAPTER XLIII.

THE HYPNOTIC SPELL.

"That fiend is slowly killing him!" It was Sunday evening, just after eight o'clock, and the little ward in which Nick Carter found himself was deserted save for its two inmates. On his bed lay James Stone, motionless and mute, just as he had lain there all through the day. Over him bent Nick, and there was a pitying look in the detective's eyes as they rested on the white face.

Dropping his hand gently on Stone's eyelids, he lifted them and looked at the set, fixed pupils. They were small, almost the size of pin heads.

"There isn't the slightest doubt about it," the detective decided, "this man is under some powerful narcotic, which means that Follansbee has his own reasons for keeping him thus. I'd give a good deal to know just what is at the bottom of it, but, after all, it doesn't greatly matter. I know that Follansbee means no good, and I'm here to see that he fails; that's the important thing."

During the day Nick had kept to his room, and the nurse, a gentle little woman, had decided that he was a model patient. He had, however, ventured to make a few inquiries about the inanimate man in the next bed, and the nurse had given him several details.

"He came from St. Swithin's," she said. "Doctor Follansbee—the head there you know—is looking after him, so he must consider it a very important case. The doctor says that he doesn't expect the patient to awaken for at least another twenty-four hours. He's in an unusual sort of coma."

There was nothing to be gained by revealing his suspicions to the nurse; therefore Nick kept his peace. He knew, however, that Follansbee would have to return again to see the man, and it was for that visit he was waiting—waiting with an impatience which proved the hold the case had upon him.

Another hour passed before Stephen Follansbee's voice warned him that the long-looked-for moment had arrived. The detective had been sitting up much of the time, but at the sound he stripped off his bath robe and jumped into bed, the nurse being absent. In a few seconds the covers were pulled up to his chin and his face was turned to the wall.

It would have taken a clever observer to notice that on the wall, almost level with his head, hung a small mirror. It had been tilted at such an angle that the detective, although he had his back to the bed occupied by Stone, could see everything that happened there.

The door opened, and he heard a soft footfall. He lay quite still, breathing easily and regularly.

There was only one light in the room, a shaded bulb, which was suspended above a small table that stood close to Stone's bed. The rest of the little ward was in semidarkness.

"Another patient?"

The detective recognized an undercurrent of disagreeable surprise, if not of anger, in Follansbee's voice.

Miss Worth had accompanied the physician into the room. "Yes, a typhoid convalescent," she answered, in a low voice. "He came last night, and there was no other place to put him. He seems to be asleep now."

Nick could hear Follansbee's footfalls as the latter came across the room and halted by the side of the bed. The hawklike face bent over him and the beady eyes searched his features for a few moments.

The pains which Nick had taken in his disguise justified themselves, however, and Follansbee presently straightened up.

"Very well, Miss Worth," he said, turning to the matron, "you need not wait. If I want the nurse I shall call her."

The woman left the ward. Nick heard the door close softly behind her, and then he cautiously opened his eyes a little and glanced up at the tilted mirror. It caught the glow from the electric bulb, and he could see every movement that the doctor made—could even mark the sinister expression on Follansbee's face. The head of St. Swithin's had been carrying a little bag, and this he placed on the table, bringing out various articles and placing them in readiness. Then, from the inside pocket, the scientific criminal withdrew a small case containing a number of glass tubes.

When his preparations were completed, Follansbee seated himself on the bed and made a swift examination of the helpless man. The expression on his face was almost fiendish now, and the lids were curled in a mocking smile. Evidently the callous scoundrel was gloating over his triumph.

Nick held his breath as he watched, for Follansbee had set to work now. The swift, capable fingers reached out toward the little table, selected one of the vials, and dropped its contents on a little pad of cotton. When the pad was saturated, the doctor bent closer over Stone in such a way that the detective was unable to see what happened; but a moment later, when Follansbee straightened up, the first sign of life appeared in the motionless figure.

The head moved restlessly from side to side and the eyes fluttered open. Very slowly Stone lifted himself up until he was in a sitting position. His eyes were wide and staring now, and he looked about him with the half-vacant expression of a dazed man.

Follansbee had stepped back as Stone sat up, and now, reseating himself on the edge of the bed, the criminal craned his lean neck forward, so that his face was on a level with that of his victim.

Stone's eyes, which had been wavering about the room, seemed to fix themselves on the hard, little ones which met them; whereupon Follansbee raised his hands and began to make passes in front of the staring, intent face.

The meaning of his actions was at once revealed to the detective: Follansbee had brought his man back to life only to hypnotize him. For what purpose?

CHAPTER XLIV.

CHICK COMES TO GRIEF.

With every nerve on the alert, Nick Carter waited.

He was prepared to interfere at once, whatever the cost, if he should feel Stone was in any immediate peril; but he was curious to hear and see all he could. Suddenly a thin voice pierced the silence.

"You are well now," it announced. "You feel your strength returning."

It was Stephen Follansbee who spoke, and the slow incisiveness of the tone seemed to cut through the stillness of the room like a knife.

"Yes. I feel it. I'm much better now—almost well."

Nick hardly recognized Stone's voice, so changed was it. It sounded thin and vague, as though the man were hardly sure of himself, as if he had been in solitary confinement for months.

It was by no means the first time that the detective had witnessed a hypnotist at work, but seldom had he experienced a more dramatic thrill than he did at that moment. The uncanny power gave him the creeps.

"To-morrow you will get up and go back to the Hotel Windermere," Follansbee went on. His eyes never left those of his victim, and he was speaking slowly and distinctly, so that the entranced brain would follow each detail.

"Remember that to-morrow is Monday," he said. "The bank people will want to see you, and you must tell them that the check for four hundred and fifty thousand dollars is quite correct—that it covers not only professional fees, but a business transaction, the nature of which you are not at liberty to reveal."

Subtle and powerful though the influence was that held the poor, abused brain in thrall, Nick saw a shaft of doubt cross Stone's face.

"The check for forty-five thousand," the miner corrected, in his far-off tone.

Follansbee's face went suddenly livid. "Not forty-five thousand!" he cried. "Four hundred and fifty thousand. Don't you remember?"

Again the clawlike hands moved in swift passes in front of the rigid features, and the doubt vanished from the reflected face as Nick watched it.

"Yes, four hundred and fifty thousand," murmured Stone mechanically, as if talking in his sleep.

An expression of exultant content possessed Stephen Follansbee's features. It was victory for him now. With this man under his complete control, ready to carry out his desires, he believed his position was secure.

If Stone appeared at the bank and authorized the transaction, the chief weapon which still remained in Nicholas Carter's grasp would be torn away.

The plotter started to get up from the bed. "You are— —" he began.

But at that moment the faint click of some hard object sounded against the glass of the window, and was accompanied by a smothered exclamation. Follansbee wheeled abruptly and peered through the opening. Outlined against the background of glass, he—and the detective as well—saw a head and shoulders.

With a swiftness that few would have given him credit for, the doctor darted across the room and threw up the sash; then his long arms shot out and closed around the intruder's throat, strangling the words that rose to his lips. The swift movement brought Nick round, and he stared at the open window out of which Follansbee was leaning, his outstretched arm thrust into the darkness.

Over the rounded shoulders the detective caught sight of a familiar face involuntarily twisted in pain. It was that of Chick Carter.

For the fraction of a second Nick found himself surprised that it was not Patsy. It would have been quite like the latter, especially after his unauthorized activities of the last few nights, to have come there to see for himself how things were going; but Chick's appearance was unlooked for.

Nick had heard and seen enough, however, and even had the interruption been far more unwelcome, he would not have remained idle. With a swift bound he was on his feet, and then, darting across the room, he hurled himself headlong at Follansbee.

He was just in time.

Patsy Garvan had talked over his affairs with Chick, and the latter had decided to accompany him to Miss Worth's hospital at the expiration of twenty-four hours. They had entered the grounds at the rear, and had made their way without detection to a point beneath the window which Patsy knew belonged to Ward E.

A stout vine climbed the wall beside the window, and Patsy had wanted to make use of it in order to gain a view of the room, but Nick's first assistant had used his authority as Patsy's senior, and made the ascent instead. The ward was on the second floor, but the ground fell away from the building on that side, and was about ten feet below the level of the main floor; consequently there was a nasty drop from the second floor to the concrete walk beneath.

The climb had been an easy matter for Chick, and no more risky than the stunts he did every day. When he had reached the level of the window sill, however, he had found the footing rather precarious. The main stem of the vine was three feet or more to the left of the window. He was obliged to hold this with his left hand and lean far out, with one foot extended along a branch of the vine. In this way he was able to get his right hand on the window sill and to pull the vine over far enough so that he could look into the window. But his efforts had loosened the vine, and when he felt it giving way, he made a sudden thoughtless move, which brought one of the buttons of his coat sleeve in sharp contact with the pane.

That was the sound Nick and Follansbee had heard.

The doctor's lightninglike attack had taken Chick by surprise, and the detective, who was clawing for a fresh hold had been unable to resist. He had let go of the vine the moment the window was opened, and had clutched the inner edge of the sill with both hands; but while he was doing so, Follansbee had secured a strangle hold, and begun to push his head backward, with the obvious intention of making him let go of the sill.

The rascally physician would have been no match for Chick under ordinary circumstances, but that situation was a different matter. The young detective was absolutely defenseless.

It was all over in a few seconds, but they seemed like years to Carter's assistant.

"A-h-h!"

It was a thin, frenzied scream that went up. Chick felt the muscular fingers relax from his throat, and dimly saw the long, lean arms, waving wildly, drawn in from the window. For a few moments he hung there, gasping, then, inch by inch he dragged himself up until his head was level with the sill again, and his feet had found a support on a little ledge which hooded the first-floor window.

Another heave brought him higher, and he dizzily drew himself over the sill somehow, anyhow, into the room. For an instant he lay where he had fallen, while the interior of the room danced about him. Then, as his eyes cleared, he saw two figures writhing on the floor, locked in each other's arms. Summoning all of his strength, and gritting his teeth, he rose to his feet and staggered forward.

It seemed as if the Fury possessed Follansbee, for he fought like a wild cat, and it was all Carter could do to hold him down. But the detective won at last, and as Chick scrambled to his feet, Follansbee was stretched out flat on his back, while the chief, with one hand on the heaving chest, pinned the miscreant to the floor.

"It looks like a—a case of handcuffs, chief," Chick said, panting for breath.

CHAPTER XLV.

"HEAVEN HELP ME."

Nick Carter looked up at his assistant's words, then nodded toward the door. "Lock that!" he commanded. "Quick!"

Chick made his way dizzily across the room and turned the key in the lock. He knew the meaning of the move. The noise of the struggle might have been heard, and if so, the room might be invaded at any moment. It was evident that the chief did not wish such an interruption. As soon as Chick had locked the door, he returned to his chief's side.

"Now, watch this fellow," the detective directed. "Don't let him make even a move to get up."

As he spoke, Nick got to his feet, and, striding to the wall, switched on a couple more lights, flooding the room.

Follansbee lay where he had been left, but his evil eyes searched the features of the pajama-clad detective. Seemingly he had guessed his identity, but had failed to verify his suspicions from the bearded face.

"Who are you?" he demanded. "And what does this mean?"

Simultaneously he started to rise on one elbow, but Chick prodded him in the ribs with his foot.

"Stay where you are!" he advised. "I have my eye on you, you know."

"It's too much trouble to take off this beard, Follansbee," Nick replied evenly. "I hardly think that's necessary, anyhow. I have a notion you could guess at my name without much trouble, and that the guess would be right. I am Nick Carter, not at yours—but at James Stone's—service."

There was a tense, dramatic silence; then suddenly, with a curious, gurgling sound, another figure came to the stage.

Stone, swinging himself out of bed, rose to his feet unsteadily. The blind, vacant look had vanished. A perplexed, troubled frown had taken its place, and Stone turned his head slowly, eying each of the occupants of the room in turn.

"What is this?" he asked, in a hesitating voice. "What does it mean?"

Follansbee screwed himself round on the floor and faced the man. Chick caught the look on the doctor's face, and guessed what he was up to.

"No, you don't," he remarked, stooping down and jerking Follansbee about by the collar. "Keep your eyes off him and cut out your Svengali tricks."

There was no doubt that Stone was coming out from the influence of the spell which had been laid upon him, but he would doubtless have succumbed again had it not been for Chick's quick move. As it was, he had already looked at Follansbee and recognized him.

The ex-miner passed his hands across his eyes. "I thought I'd seen the last of you," he jerked out. "I remember leaving your house, but after that—after that——"

His voice faltered and broke, and his look was pathetic as he turned toward Nick Carter.

"I seem to recognize you," he went on. "I wonder if you are my friend. Can you explain?"

A look of hope sprang into the detective's eyes, and he nodded his head eagerly.

"I think I can," he answered. "You have been made a victim of a cold-blooded rascal. I need not tell you what happened at the Hotel Windermere, I suppose?"

James Stone's awakening memory brought the scene back to him, and he shuddered.

"I know—I know," he said, dropping back quickly on the side of his bed. "I—I tried to murder poor old Win. But you saved me from that, didn't you?"

He looked appealingly at Follansbee. The latter could no longer bear his ignominious position on the floor. With a look of defiance he scrambled to his feet, and Carter and his assistant allowed him to do so, although they ranged themselves on either side of him.

Follansbee knew that he was in desperate straits, but he believed that his star was not yet ready to set. He made one mistake, however; for he imagined that Winthrop Crawford had been inoculated with the deadly disease.

"You are mistaken," he said daringly. "By this time Crawford must be suffering from the disease that you placed in his veins."

"No, no, no! You don't mean that—you can't mean it!" Stone broke out, in a horrified voice. "You told me that the syringe was filled with a harmless liquid."

"That was a lie," was the brutal answer.

A groan burst from the lips of the tall man, and his lean figure seemed to shrivel. "Then Heaven help me!" he moaned. "I've killed the man I love best in the world."

"No, you have not!"

CHAPTER XLVI.

THE BOND IS MENDED.

Crisply, cuttingly, the words came from Nick Carter's lips, and Follansbee wheeled on him in a flash.

"It was no fault of Follansbee that you did not carry out the vile scheme his cunning brain had devised," Nick went on. "I was fortunately able to thwart him and to thwart your irresponsible aims of the moment at the same time."

Then, in quiet tones, the detective told the whole story, which was listened to in a breathless silence by the others.

"At this moment," the detective concluded, "Winthrop Crawford is perfectly well, and is looking forward eagerly to meeting his old friend again."

"You—you mean that he forgives me?"

"I do," was the reassuring answer. "He has forgiven you again and again because he knew you were not yourself, and because he's one man in ten thousand."

Stephen Follansbee's sharp voice cut in. "This is all very interesting," he said sarcastically, "but you will oblige me, Carter, by unlocking that door and letting me go my way."

The two men measured glances for a moment.

"Do you imagine that you have sufficient evidence against me?" Follansbee went on cynically. "If you do, you're destined to meet with a shock. Don't forget that you may have to bring both of these men into it along with me, especially Stone—for, by your own statement, it was he who attempted to kill his partner."

The detective turned to Stone.

"A check signed by you for the sum of four hundred and fifty thousand dollars, payable to this man, was presented at the bank yesterday, and cashed. Do you know anything about it?"

The miner lifted his head.

"No, no! I made out a check, but it was only forty-five thousand. That was bad enough, but—what day is this?"

"This is Sunday, the twenty-sixth," Nick answered.

"Then my check cannot have been cashed," Stone said, with a great sigh of relief. "You must be mistaken, for I distinctly remember that I dated it the twenty-seventh."

"In that case, Mr. Stone," said Nick, "you have a chance of getting even with this fellow. I made no mistake in saying that he cashed a check for four hundred and fifty thousand dollars yesterday, but it was dated the twenty-fifth. Circumstances have conspired with his own cunning to save him from the charge of being an accessory to a murder, but he won't find it so easy to avoid the consequences of this other crime. We can't accuse him of forgery, because the signature is evidently yours, but we can make out a complete check-raising case against him without the slightest trouble. A peculiar kind of 'disappearing ink' was used. I've already brought out your original writing in one place, Stone, and I can bring out all of it by the same process. That will doubtless corroborate you as to the amount and date—and Stephen Follansbee will come off his perch."

The famous specialist gave a peculiar strangled sound in his throat and his hands dropped to his side.

"You've won, Carter," he said, his voice quavering. "I'll return the money—every cent of it, if you will drop the case—and you will have to do that. The whole thing will come out if you try to press it, and Stone will be branded as a man who was once under treatment for insanity."

"You're right, Follansbee, in part," Nick told him quietly. "I've won, and the time has come for you to throw down your arms. Don't be too sure about the rest, though. I don't believe my friend Stone here has any desire to let you go free, if he can be shown a way to prevent it. Isn't that right, Stone?"

"It certainly is," was the emphatic response. "If it is a possible thing to make this infernal scamp pay for what he has done, I say go ahead, by all means; but I don't see how——"

"It's my business to find a way," Nick interrupted, "and I think I have."

"How?" Stone eagerly demanded.

"By keeping this fact in mind," the chief explained: "Follansbee isn't going to bite off his nose to spite his face. He says that everything will come out, but that's nonsense, and he knows it. We have a clear case against him, and we can press it without lugging in anything that we don't want to be spread on the records. All the judge and jury need to know is that you went to Follansbee for professional advice and treatment—it doesn't matter for what. His lawyers will know that the case is going against him, anyway, and all their energies will be directed toward obtaining as light a sentence as possible. That being so, they will be very careful to keep quiet about the nature of the trouble that brought you to him."

"I don't see why," confessed Stone.

"It's perfectly obvious," Nick insisted. "Any decent lawyer would know that Follansbee would get a much more severe sentence if it came out that he had attempted to victimize an irresponsible man; to swindle one who was temporarily incompetent, and take away practically his entire fortune. That would be the last straw."

"I see!" Stone cried excitedly. "It would be even more to the interest of the defense to keep dark on that subject than it would for the prosecution."

"Then you will get satisfaction, as well as your money back," Nick told him confidently; and then added to the cowed wretch at his side: "The jig is up, Follansbee. I won't lock you up until you turn over your loot; but you may as well write out your resignation as head of St. Swithin's, and your millionaire patients will have to hunt for some one else to doctor them. You will find it inconvenient to discharge your professional duties in a cell."

Apparently the detective plucked a pair of handcuffs from the air, and, before Follansbee knew what was happening, they were snapped on his wrists.

A few hours later—some time after midnight—two bronzed men met and clasped hands in Nick Carter's study. They did not say much at first, but the detective's heart swelled as he watched them.

The partners had been reunited, and the broken bond had been welded anew.

THE END.

Lector House believes that a society develops through a two-fold approach of continuous learning and adaptation, which is derived from the study of classic literary works spread across the historic timeline of literature records. Therefore, we aim at reviving, repairing and redeveloping all those inaccessible or damaged but historically as well as culturally important literature across subjects so that the future generations may have an opportunity to study and learn from past works to embark upon a journey of creating a better future.

This book is a result of an effort made by Lector House towards making a contribution to the preservation and repair of original ancient works which might hold historical significance to the approach of continuous learning across subjects.

HAPPY READING & LEARNING!

LECTOR HOUSE LLP
E-MAIL: lectorpublishing@gmail.com